A GENTLEMAN OF MYSTERY

THE BLUESTOCKING SCANDALS BOOK 8

ELLIE ST. CLAIR

CONTENTS

THE ART OF STEALING A DUKE'S HEART

Facebook: Ellie St. Clair

Cover by AJF Designs

Do you love historical romance? Receive access to a free ebook, as well as exclusive content such as giveaways, contests, freebies and advance notice of pre-orders through my mailing list!

Sign up here!

Also By Ellie St. Clair

The Bluestocking Scandals
Designs on a Duke
Inventing the Viscount
Discovering the Baron
The Valet Experiment
Writing the Rake
Risking the Detective
A Noble Excavation
A Gentleman of Mystery

For a full list of all of Ellie's books, please see
www.elliestclair.com/books.

CHAPTER 1

LONDON ~ 1824 ~ THREE WEEKS BEFORE ROSE'S
WEDDING

*H*e moved not a muscle yet knew he wasn't still.

He was rocking. Back and forth, up and down, side to side. He was going to be sick.

How was it possible? He attempted to pry open his eyes, tried to sit up, but an icy vise enclosed his body, held his lids closed, rendered him immobile.

There was a shout, and the rocking stopped. He was still again, until hands came beneath his shoulders, and he was moving once more, but this time not in the gentle motion of the waves but a rough lifting movement, as though he was a pack of goods.

Panic gripped him.

Where was he? Who had him? What were they doing with him?

"What do we have here?" A voice, a faraway voice, drifted down toward him like a gentle, calming breeze, followed by a response that was a mixture of rough grunts coming from close to him. Hard wood hit his back. It was cold and damp, and he shivered, wishing he was somewhere else. Perhaps in front of a warm fire. Under a blanket. He tried to picture what home looked like, of the place he was supposed to be, but he couldn't capture the image in his mind.

Why?

"Don't leave him lying there," came the voice again, this time clearer, closer. "Bring him up to the cart."

He was jostled again, carried up toward something, to someone, although to what or where, or whom, he had no idea.

He was dropped down again, and while his bed was still hard and rough, it was not quite so cold, as though there was a layer between him and whatever plank surface was beneath.

When he shivered, a warm hand came to his face, in such contrast to his own temperature that it nearly burned him.

"We need to hurry. He's too cold."

That voice again. It soothed the rising tumult in his chest, for some strange reason providing him the assurance that everything was going to be all right.

How, he had no idea.

His mind was foggy, but all he could see, all he could remember, was thrashing about in the water. There must have been an explosion and the next thing he knew he was fighting against the waves that crashed over him, attempting to take him down within their icy depths. He had fought until he had realized that fighting was the last thing he should be doing, that the only way to survive was to be one with the waves, to allow them to take him, to carry him wherever they chose to go.

He had found relief when a solid board had met his

fingers. He recalled using every ounce of his strength to haul himself on top of the piece of floating debris.

Then everything had gone black once more.

Now here he was, immobile, incapable of doing anything more than lying here, at the whim of these people who had him within their grasp.

"Rest. You're going to be all right."

That voice, calming him once more, caused him to still his tense muscles as they attempted movement. Surely people who intended him harm would not treat him with such kindness? Would not take the time to speak to him with such warmth?

He could smell the salt of the ocean and the rot of river, although whether it was coming from a nearby body of water or from his own self, he had no idea. It could have been a mixture of the two. Besides the shouts around him, he could hear far off cries, noises of people — on roads, in buildings, calling to one another, traveling from one place to the next.

Had he been one of those people? Had he known where he was going, what his purpose had been? He wasn't sure, but one thing he knew — he was not meant to be this man, this man who was at the mercy of others, who had no control over his surroundings let alone his own body.

He was supposed to be the man telling others what to do, the man in charge.

"Who is he?"

He wished he could answer her, but his tongue felt heavy, a foreign object in his mouth, one that he could not seem to properly move to form any words, while his throat was so dry, so parched that he could hardly swallow let alone make any sound.

"I think he's trying to speak." Another voice. Male this time.

"Water. Get water."

That burning hand came to the back of his neck and she gently lifted his head, just far enough.

"Drink if you can."

Something hard came to his lips, and at the slightest touch of water, he no longer needed to think nor worry as his body knew what to do and began searching for more, suddenly desperate for the cooling solace of the liquid.

"Slow now. Don't want to make yourself sick."

He resisted being ordered about, but was incapable of doing otherwise as the hands holding him controlled what he received.

He needed to get up. Needed to get out of here.

"What's this now?"

The hands placed his head back down on the surface below him, and were now at his neck, running over bare skin, stroking him with their fire.

They must have found something, for a weight from his neck was suddenly lifted.

"It's a medallion of some kind."

"Oh? Say anything?"

"It does."

No. The panic overwhelmed him again. He didn't know why, but deep within him, he was well aware that no one could know who he was. He had to protect — himself? Someone else? He didn't know, but he knew he had to hide, to seek out safety, or all could be lost.

He tried to lift his hand, to push the fingers away before anything about him could be discovered — as desperately as he longed to know the truth himself.

"Leopold. It says Leopold."

And just like that, his eyes flew open in recognition. Finally, something made sense. Something fit. He had an answer.

But any threads of remembrance quickly fell away at the vision before him.

A face. Her face. He didn't need to remember what home looked like anymore.

For he had found it.

* * *

GEORGIE NEARLY FELL BACK on her heels when he opened his eyes.

They were the most intriguing shade of blue-green she had ever seen. They reminded her of a clear pond on a sunny day — nothing at all like the murky river they had pulled the stranger from.

He was in distress, that was obvious. She knew he had been trying to move, would likely have fled if he had the ability to do so. All of the finely toned muscles of his body tensed beneath his ripped clothing, while he shivered nearly uncontrollably. His lips were already turning an inhuman shade of blue that was eerily close to many of the cadavers Georgie had seen pulled from the very same river.

The other two detectives with her, Marshall and Frank, were moving far too slowly for her liking. They were pulling in the board the man must have drifted in on, looking about for any other signs of where he had come from or just what might have happened to him.

"Must have been from the explosion earlier today," Marshall muttered, looking out over the Thames as though it held all of the answers.

"But all of the men were accounted for," Frank argued, and Marshall shrugged.

"Where else would he come from?"

Georgie ignored their bickering, looking down to find that the stranger was still watching her, and she shook her head as she knew she needed to release herself from his stare that had rendered her immobile.

"You're all right," she said, releasing the medallion she held in her hand back to his chest. "We'll get you to a hospital and warmed up in no time."

She didn't say anything about the blood that matted his hair, nor the visible protrusion below it. How he had survived such a blow was nearly inconceivable, but then, she had seen stranger things before.

At her words, a flare of panic flashed in his eyes, and in a sudden, halting yet impressive feat of strength, his arms lifted, his hands flying up to grasp her arms over the sleeves of her black jacket.

"No," he growled out, his voice hoarse through his parched throat. "You can't."

"No?" She lifted a brow. So he had gotten himself on the wrong side of the law then. She tamped down the trickle of disappointment. Beneath the filth, he seemed a fine specimen of a man, that was for certain, but what did it matter to her who he was or what he had done? He was a case. A call. Nothing that meant anything to her.

Yet somehow, she sensed that he was holding onto her as a lifeline, trusting her to ensure that he found safety and solace.

"You can't take me there. It would kill me."

"A hospital? Why?"

"I don't know."

She eyed him warily, trying to determine if what he said was true. She had met many a liar, but from the panic that stormed through his eyes, she had the sense that he believed in what he said.

"You don't know," she repeated incredulously.

"I don't," he rasped. "I just know that my life is threatened, and to go there… I can't tell you how I know that I mustn't. I just know."

Georgie stared at him, reading the hard planes of his face. He had a distinguished look to him, prominent cheekbones and a patrician nose beneath the bruises and wan skin tone from his time in the water.

His hair was wet, dirty, but from what she could tell, it was a dark blond, speckled with dark strands.

Just as he didn't seem to understand how he knew what he knew, in the same breath she was aware that what he spoke of was true — or, at the very least, he believed it to be.

"Very well," she muttered. "I don't know why I should believe you, but I do."

Relief crossed his face, and at her words, his eyes slid closed once more and he rested his head back against the bed of the cart beneath him.

"Are we ready?" Marshall ambled over, an eyebrow raised, and Georgie nodded at him.

"We are."

She climbed down from the cart, pulling Marshall over to the side. He was one of her closest friends, and while he was not always the best of Bow Street's detectives, he was solid and steady, always someone she could count on. His wife often invited her over for dinner, and Georgie considered his children to be like her own nieces and nephews.

"We can't take him to the hospital."

"Why not?" Marshall asked, hands on his hips, and Georgie was well aware that he was looking forward to putting the day behind him and returning to his family.

"He says his life is in danger."

"It will be if we don't get him some medical help soon."

"I know," she said, lifting her cap and scratching at the curls beneath it. She knew her life would be easier if she cut them all off, but it was the one piece of vanity that she held onto. "But Marshall... the panic in his eyes when I told him where we were going, his relief when I promised him I wouldn't take him there... I can't tell you why I know it would be wrong to do so. I just know it would be."

"Georgie," Marshall said, shaking his head at her. "He's not a lost little puppy. The man could be a criminal."

"If he is, he is too incapacitated to do anything about it. His clothing is modest, but that medal he's wearing around his neck, it's made of the finest of silver. He's been through something, that's for sure, but he's got a look of wealth to him."

"Which means he could be one of the worst. If we don't take him to the hospital, just what do you suggest we do with him?"

Georgie took a breath. She knew Marshall wasn't going to like this, but she didn't see any other option.

"I will take him home."

CHAPTER 2

*H*e woke to the warmth of flames watching over him, their billowing, just beyond his reach, casting a comforting embrace over his body, which was now bare down to the waist, a blanket over his lower half preserving some modesty.

As he cracked open his eyes and looked down, he wondered just who had undressed him. All he could recall from the last time he had opened his eyes was the face of his angel, his saviour, looking down upon him. While he was well aware he should be questioning where — and *who* — he was, he found himself wondering instead about who the woman was and just where she might be now.

He tried to sit up, but winced as first his head began pounding, around his ears and then down to the base, where he had obviously hit it upon something, although what, he had no idea.

He couldn't remember.

He couldn't remember anything.

Cool metal flowed across his chest, and he lifted his hand

to find a smooth, silver chain around his neck, the circular pendant in the middle.

Leopold.

That's right.

He remembered from the docks now, the angel reading his pendant in that smooth voice of hers, one that was filled with exuberance and that he knew would be full of light and laughter in other circumstances.

Other circumstances than pulling a half-drowned man out of the water.

A series of images came crashing down into his consciousness, and he winced as he brought his hand to his temple, using it to try to ward away the pain of the moments that seemed to have neither connection nor meaning yet told him enough.

There was a flash of light. A crack of sound. A circle of men. Then the splash of water.

And a threat. He remembered a threat.

It was the same sequence that had come to him when they had pulled him onto the docks, that he had remembered after he had seen the woman's face.

He knew someone was after him. He couldn't say why he knew not to go to anywhere that someone might find him. But somehow, deep within him, he was aware that his identity needed to remain as forgotten by everyone around him as it was by himself.

With a grunt, he lifted himself up on his elbows, looking around the room he was in through the haze that covered his vision.

It was sparse, clean, and yet was filled with… comfort.

A painting against the door that was clearly amateur but was colored with an enthusiastic stroke.

Well-used blankets draped over the furniture. Tea sets and dishes that were not just for show lined the tables beside stacks of books that were obviously read, not meant to impress.

The room was small, but was centered around the hearth in front of which he was lying, on a bed of blankets and pillows that held him in their softness.

A bouquet of flowers picked from the wild added lively purple and green near the doorway, and while Leo — yes, Leo, that sounded right — wouldn't have said the room held much of a feminine touch, it most certainly belonged to someone who understood how to make a house into a home.

The door to the outside was closed, but a small corridor led down a short hall. A figure passed in front of the door — a man, though a rather slight one, who had removed his jacket and was now walking about in a linen shirt and blue waistcoat.

Leo tried to call out, to ask for a drink of water, but his voice was rusty from disuse and seawater.

He leaned back, accepting defeat for a moment as he closed his eyes, the room going dark. Just a moment of rest and then he would force himself up to walk around and find something to drink.

Just one more moment.

* * *

GEORGIE PERCHED on the edge of her sofa and stared down at the man — Leopold. He was far more handsome than any man had the right to be, and she couldn't stop her eyes from following the lines of his hard, defined tanned chest, slightly dusted with golden hair, over the rigid abdomen and down the trail that led below the blanket Marshall had placed overtop of the man's still-wet breeches before he had shaken his head at Georgie and then left for the night.

He had made it more than clear that he wholeheartedly

disapproved of this arrangement, and that once Drake, their colleague, learned of what was occurring, he would be on her doorstep in moments.

Georgie had to use every bribe and piece of blackmail she had on Marshall to convince him not to say anything to a soul — especially Drake. Not now. He had a new wife and had been through enough himself that he didn't need to add any of Georgie's problems to that list, no matter how close of friends they might be. If the time came that she needed him, she would call on him. But until then, she had this handled.

She had finally won Marshall over when she had told him that if he said a thing, she would tell his wife just exactly what Marshall really thought of her blackberry scones.

That had been enough to shut him up.

She grinned triumphantly once more. The truth was, it wasn't hard to triumph over Marshall, but it was always satisfying never the less.

Now she returned her attention to the man she had been left with.

She couldn't help the flicker of trepidation that coursed through her belly as she stared at him. Despite the fact he couldn't be more demure at the moment, as incapacitated as he was, he intimidated her.

And Georgie was never intimidated.

She looked into the fire, cheered by its warmth, before something called her to look back toward him.

His eyes were open.

Staring.

That beautiful sea-green cut deep within her, as though they could see through her, knowing each thought that passed through her mind. Which she knew was ridiculous. There was nothing to see.

"You're awake."

She stated the obvious, and he only blinked. He opened

his mouth, but when nothing came out but a grunt, she leapt to her feet, immediately realizing what he needed.

"You must want water."

His eyebrows furrowed for a moment as though he was going to argue, but then he nodded curtly, and she hurried over to the side of the room to the pitcher, even as she tried to tell herself that she was not running from his inscrutable stare.

Georgie was never speechless. She was never flummoxed. And she certainly never ran from any man.

She wasn't going to start now.

She was simply getting water for him.

She crossed the room with glass in hand, mindful of him watching her before looking around the room, assessing her and the small rooms she rented, that she had made her home for two years now.

For a time she had lived with another woman — a seamstress — but she was glad that she had decided to live on her own since Moira had gotten married. It allowed her the chance for independence — and the opportunity to host handsome strangers.

She snorted inwardly. Not that she had ever actually done so before now. She was glad, at least, that she had decided to change into more feminine attire, although why it would matter, she had no idea.

"Here you are," she said, leaning over and placing a hand behind his head as she helped him lift it to drink. He did so greedily, and she had to take the glass away, knowing what would happen if he gulped it down too quickly.

He wrenched his head back and looked at her with an intensity that seemed to come from deep within his soul.

"Stronger."

"Stronger?" she asked, taken aback by how deep his voice was. It was a smooth caress, a low near-bass that strummed a chord deep within, urging her to lie back and listen to him read anything — even the minutes of the last session of Parliament if need be — as long as it meant he wouldn't stop talking.

"Do you have any brandy?" he asked. "Or does your husband?"

She lifted her eyebrows at the assumption, but didn't correct him. She supposed that if he did happen to be a man who could possibly murder her in her bed, it was better that the thought, for now, at least until he could assess for himself otherwise, that there was a man here.

Although the truth was, she could protect herself just fine.

"I have whiskey."

"That will do."

She nodded succinctly, pouring a very short glass for both of them before walking over and handing it to him, surprised when she turned around to find that he was now sitting up, leaning back against the sofa.

"You must be feeling better."

He nodded, but then winced.

"All fine except this head."

"You need a physician."

"I'm fine."

"Here," she said, taking a sip before placing the whiskey down on the table beside her. "Let me have a look."

She bent over him, trying to ignore the tingle of awareness that danced over her skin and down her spine as she felt every sensation that sprang from him — his breath on her arm, the tension with which he held his head, the intensity of his gaze as it looked her up and down.

She knew what he saw. A woman who was too tall, too broad, her features too strong and prominent to be anything one might admire in a woman.

But that didn't matter.

She was helping him as any Bow Street constable would have done.

Although most constables probably couldn't have been convinced by a handsome countenance and a desperate plea to take him home.

She was a fool. But it was too late now to retract her decision.

Georgie ran her hands over the silk of his hair, wondering if it was truly such a dark blond or if it was the dirt of his ordeal that had caused it to be so. One thing was for certain — the blood that was caked near the base of his skull certainly added an unnatural color to it.

"You've got quite the gash here," she murmured, forgetting for a moment how she was reacting to his nearness as she assessed the injury to the back of his head. "You must have lost a lot of blood. Probably why you're feeling so weak."

"I'm not weak," he muttered. "Just tired."

"Mm hmm," she said, not commenting any further, for clearly this was a source of pride for him. Her assessment complete, she sat back, remaining on the floor with him, although she scooted backward to lean against the wall next to the hearth, enjoying the heat thrown by the fire. "I still think you need a physician. I don't know much about head injuries."

"I'll be fine once my memory comes back."

She shook her head incredulously at him. "Is that what you think? That your memories are going to come rushing back in a flood? I'm not sure that's how it works."

He frowned. "They'll come back at some point. They have to."

She looked down, realizing that he didn't currently have the capacity to accept the fact that he might never remember who he was, that he might have to start life anew. She had seen it before. He hadn't been the first man to wash up on the shores of the Thames, and he wouldn't be the last. Too many of them had waited for years for someone to come and "claim" them, but had remained disappointed.

"At least you know your name." She pointed to the medallion that fit far too perfectly into the grooves on his chest. "Leopold."

"Yes," he said. "I think I prefer Leo."

"Leo." She nodded slowly. "It suits. Do you remember anything else?"

"No," he said, but she could tell he was keeping something from her, as he twisted his head to the side.

"You're lying."

"I'm not."

"You are," she said, although without any malice. "I can always tell when someone is lying."

"That's a bold statement."

"It's the truth," she said, the corners of her mouth quirking up. "That, you can be sure of."

He snorted, crossing his arms over his chest.

"Besides," she continued, "how else would you have known you were in danger?"

His expression darkened. "I just *know*. I have only a few flashes of memories. Moments, really. And… it's stupid."

"Try telling me anyway."

"I am worried that whoever I am with is in danger. Which would include you."

"I can handle myself."

"Since we've now covered the total sum of what I remember about who I am," he said, lifting his head, his stare piercing across the short distance to where she sat on the floor across from him now, "tell me, just who are you, and what am I doing in your home?"

CHAPTER 3

*S*he swallowed at his question, looking down so that
he could no longer see her face.

A pity. He liked looking at her face.

He liked it far too much.

When she had entered the room, her stare had washed
over him like the basking of the sun.

Which was ridiculous. He was a grown man, of that he
was aware, and he had no business being so enraptured by a
woman he didn't even know.

But here he was, unable to even look away from her.

"What's your name?" he insisted, needing to know, rueing
whatever man was hiding beyond the corridor, waiting for
her in their bedchamber.

"Georgie."

"That's a man's name."

She swung her head back up toward him, and he was
rewarded for his insolence by her attention one more, as
annoyed as she seemed to be.

"It is short for Georgina."

"Georgina." He allowed her name to roll over his tongue. He liked it there. "A beautiful name."

She snorted, and he smiled at the unladylike reaction.

"It doesn't suit me. Georgie does, though."

"I feel that it's hardly proper to call you by your given name. What is your last name?"

She laughed again, eyeing him with one brow crooked upward. "Georgina Jenkins, but everyone calls me Georgie, so you might as well do so. Seems you are a toff, after all."

"Pardon me?"

"We guessed that you could be a man of title. There's that silver medallion around your neck, and the way you speak now confirms it."

He nodded slowly, agreeing with her, before looking down at himself.

"Speaking of my clothes…" he lifted one corner of his lips in a slow grin, hoping to set her off balance, and while she seemed to be able to keep her head fairly well, she couldn't hide the pink flush that rose from her neck, staining her cheeks.

"Nothing much remained of your shirt," she said in answer to his unspoken question. "I'm sorry, but it's gone. We'll find something else for you. As for your trousers — there is another pair by the fire. You can change yourself when you feel up to it."

"You didn't want to help me?"

Her eyes widened in shock, but she was no simpering miss. She turned the weight of her gaze upon him.

"Are you attempting to seduce me, my lord?"

"You don't know that I'm a lord."

"I have a pretty good idea," she said wryly, "especially now that I have spoken with you."

He couldn't help but laugh at that, and the sound seemed rusty to his own ears, even though he had no idea why that would be so. What kind of man was he, that he was so unused to his own laughter? Did he even want to find out?

"How long am I welcome to stay here?" he asked, turning serious as he tilted his head to study her.

"I'm not entirely sure. You are the one who told me you were in danger, do you not recall?"

"That I do remember. Not much else, though, I'm afraid."

"It's the head injury," she said with a sigh. "I'm going to call for the physician, whether you like it or not. I know a man. He's a friend of mine and he'll be discreet. If you don't take care, you could end up dead anyway."

He may not entirely like what she had to say, but he did appreciate her straightforwardness.

"Very well."

"Truly? You're going to listen to me?"

"I just said I would, did I not?"

They held one another's stare for a moment, and he knew that this woman was not one he would ever be able to cow.

"I shall be back," she said, rising from the chair, and he ran his gaze down her frame. She wore a navy-blue dress, simple, unembellished, that cut in underneath her breasts and flowed over her body. He could see the muscle in her arms, and knew inherently that the rest of her would be equally as strong. She followed his gaze, seeming to shrink into herself when she noted his scrutiny as she swirled her cloak around to drape over her back. He had the sense she was hiding herself from him, although why, he had no idea.

"Don't go anywhere," she commanded him before she was out, into the darkness beyond, before he could even answer her.

* * *

19

GEORGIE ALLOWED the cool night air to wash over her like a balm as she quickly walked toward the physician's house, her boots moving at a fast clip over the pavement.

She was actually relieved to get out of her small set of rooms. It was too close, too uncomfortable, too hot with *him* there with her. He was so large, so intense, that he seemed to take up the entire room, and with his presence, her clothing felt too tight, her breathing was too restricted, and she needed the excuse of an escape.

She knocked on the door not far from her own Cheapside rooms, which were on the ground floor of a building she shared with four other women who had successfully become self-sufficient in London.

It swung open to reveal a woman her own age, a child attached to her leg.

"Georgie!"

"Nan, how are you tonight?"

"Just fine. Come in, come in."

Georgie nodded her thanks and stepped into the small home, immediately basking in the smell of the stew over the fire, the sound of children's voices calling to one another, the chaos of tiny bodies flying around the table. She smiled to herself as the sense of family immediately washed over her.

"Georgina Jenkins, I'm hoping this is a social visit, but I'm fearful that will never be the case."

"Carson," she turned to the voice with a smile for the man who had become a friend along with his family since they had met when they were still practically children. "It's good to see you."

He arched an eyebrow. "But?"

"You're right. I've a man who needs some attending to."

Some of the action around her paused at her words, and Nan stopped the quick cleanup she had surreptitiously started upon Georgie's arrival to stare at her. "*You* have a man?"

"Is that so hard to believe?" Georgie asked, placing her hands on her hips defensively, but then threw back her head and laughed when a guilty look crossed Nan's face.

"Oh, I'm just teasing you, Nan. You're right, he's not actually *my* man. Although, I suppose I did find him."

"You've a tendency to pick up these strays," Carson said from the door.

"I'm not sure I'd call him a stray," she began, wondering just how to describe the situation without giving too much away.

"How hurt is he?" Carson asked with a frown, even as he was already filling a bag with various instruments.

"It's a head injury, so I couldn't be certain," Georgie said, leaning back against the solid wooden table in the middle of the room. "He sustained a fairly good gash and I suspect he lost quite a bit of blood, although it's hard to tell as he was then sent for a swim."

"Please tell me he was not in the Thames."

"He was," she confirmed, to which Carson groaned.

"Thames injuries never fair well."

"Good thing I've the best physician in London coming to see him."

Carson sighed.

"You give me too much credit, Georgie."

"Or not enough. And this one should be able to pay you enough to make up for all the people you've been seeing without expectations of payment."

"Georgie…"

"Oh, don't pretend you don't. I am well aware of what you do for all these people who come to you, paying you in bread and vegetables and whatever other wares they have to sell. You don't make back nearly half of what you're owed."

21

He sighed, exchanging a look with Nan as he ran a hand through his hair.

"How am I supposed to turn away sick and injured children from my door? I just imagine how it would feel if that were my own."

"I understand, and you're a good man for it. But anyway, this one is a wealthy lord of some sort."

"Who is he?"

"Well, that's just the thing," she hedged. "I'm not entirely sure — and neither is he."

* * *

LEO WAS DISAPPOINTED in himself for just how pleased he was when he heard the door open. He told himself it was because he was relieved that she had returned unscathed from the dark hours of whatever neighborhood they happened to find themselves in, but he was chagrined to have to admit that it was more than that.

He was hanging to her with as much desperation as he had to that piece of wood he had floated upon in the water. He didn't like needing her — he didn't like needing *anyone*, he could tell — and he'd best gather his wits together before he did something stupid.

Not only was she spoken for, but he didn't know who he was or what responsibilities he had, or who might be depending on him, waiting for him to come home.

He didn't *think* he had a wife waiting for him. He felt he would know if there was a connection there, wouldn't he? Although that didn't necessarily mean that he wasn't married, of that he was aware.

"You're back."

"I'm back. And this is Mr. Swanson. He's a physician."

"Mr. Swanson," Leo said, nodding his head in greeting.

"This is—"

"A friend," Leo finished for her, not wanting to share even his first name with a stranger, despite that this Swanson was a friend of Georgie's.

"Very well," Mr. Swanson said, although Leo thought his expression contained some suspicion as he opened his bag and motioned Leo forward. "Can you walk?"

"I can," he confirmed, causing Georgie's head to swiftly rise toward him.

"You walked by yourself?"

"I was thirsty, and your husband didn't seem to have any cause to come check on me."

The doctor looked up from his tools toward Georgie.

"Your hus—"

She shook her head so slightly that Leo nearly missed it, but then a corner of his lip rose. So the woman was lying to him. Interesting.

"Come to the table, if you can," the physician said, motioning him forward toward the small two-person dining table, and Leo nodded, rising.

He had obviously overestimated his current ability, however, and in his attempt to appear uninjured, he stumbled and nearly fell over onto the sofa.

But Georgie was there to catch him. She was underneath his arm with the quickness of a cat, and she pulled one of his arms over her shoulders to help him balance.

He couldn't help but notice that it fit perfectly, as though it was meant to be there.

"Well, if there is one thing we have determined, you are both stubborn and proud," she said, and he couldn't help but grin at her.

"Maybe I'm just doing this to bring you close."

She seemed surprised at his words, but didn't respond as she led him over to the chair the doctor had motioned to.

"Sit."

Leo did as she said, and allowed the doctor to begin his examination. He hadn't wanted to admit it — to himself, or to Georgie, but he was slightly concerned at just what the man might determine. What if Leo didn't remember who he was? What if he never discovered who was out to kill him? What if he was putting Georgie in danger and didn't even know it?

What if Georgie was not who she said she was?

He pushed that last thought away even as it entered his mind. Here she was helping him, and he was only believing the very worst of her.

"So, doc?" he said finally, after not hearing anything. "Will I make it?"

"You have quite the wound," the man murmured, coming around to sit in front of Leo, pushing his too-long straight brown hair out of his eyes. He seemed to be about Leo's age, and Leo couldn't say exactly why, but he felt the man could be trusted. He seemed steady, patient, non-judgmental — just as a physician ought to be. Leo couldn't say why, but he had the feeling that his experience with physicians in the past were a far cry from this man. "It's not only a deep gash, but then the water got to it."

Leo nodded.

"Georgie says you've lost some memories."

"Mostly all of them."

The physician looked over at Georgie before returning his even gaze to Leo.

"Unfortunately, there's not much I can do but tell you to rest and keep an eye on the wound."

"That's not much help, doc."

"We can put a paste on it, see if that helps speed the healing."

He took a few things out of his bag as Georgie passed him

a bowl. He went to work, pouring and mixing before adding a bit of water. When he finished, he walked toward Leo to apply it.

"I'll do it."

Georgie stood abruptly and took the paste from the doctor, who levelled a questioning gaze at her before nodding and passing the bowl over to her.

She must have realized curiosity followed her, as she continued, "since I'll be the one applying it going forward, best I make sure I'm doing it right." She circled behind Leo, dipping her hand in the bowl and beginning to stroke it over the back of his head.

He stilled.

Her touch — even above the foul-smelling paste that coated her fingers — incited something within him.

A small ember lit deep within his belly, and he had to close his eyes as he fought against the sensation.

The sensation to turn around, take those fingers off his head, and press them against his chest.

He wanted her.

But not only did he not know anything about her — he didn't even know himself.

CHAPTER 4

Georgie could hardly breathe as she stared down at Leo's strong back.

She was barely touching him — her fingers simply placing the paste upon his head — but it was as though by making this connection with him, she had started something that she had no idea how to continue, let alone finish.

After a brief pause in which she immediately stilled at the shock of the connection between them, she slathered on the rest of the paste so quickly that he flinched beneath her administrations. When she released the bowl onto the table, it clattered so loudly, it was like someone had cracked a whip through the tension in the air. She let out her breath as she backed away quickly, before taking a heavy seat in the other chair.

"Georgie?" Carson said with a lifted brow as he stared at one of them and then the other. "A word before I go?"

She nodded jerkily as she followed him toward the door. He let himself out into the night air, and she followed without a look back at the man behind her.

Once they were outside, Carson turned his normally steady stare upon her.

"What in the hell is going on in there?"

"What do you mean?" she asked, feigning innocence.

"You know perfectly well what I mean. You and this man? Who is he and what is he doing here? I can't leave you alone with him overnight."

"Carson," she said in as steady a voice as she could, lifting a hand and placing it upon his shoulder. "I appreciate your concern. Truly, I do. But I know what I'm doing. He needs my help, and yes, I will admit that I feel some kind of... attraction toward him." Her face burned at the admission, but Carson deserved an explanation. "But not to worry. It is entirely one-sided."

"That's not the impression I received in there."

"Oh, Carson," she said with a laugh that sounded forced even to her own ears, and she could tell Carson wasn't fooled. "There is no way a man like that thinks anything of me besides perhaps some question of who I am and what I am doing with him. I saw the way he looked at me earlier. The same shock as everyone else that a woman might be built more similarly to a man than someone of her own sex. He has no idea who he is. He likely has a wife at home." Why did the thought cause such an odd ache in her gut? "He *is*, however, in danger, and I promised him a safe place to stay, at least until he remembers who he is."

"And what if he doesn't remember?" Carson pressed. "What if he is not the man you think he is? What if he tries something with you tonight?"

She wasn't about to tell Carson that the thought was not at all unwelcome but actually caused a streak of desire to lace through her entire body.

"I can take care of myself," she assured him. "Not to

worry. Now, thank you for coming. Go home to your wife and children."

"Georgie—"

"Carson." She smiled at him, put both hands on each of his shoulders, and then turned him around. "Go. I will let you know what happens on the morrow."

He looked back at her over his shoulder.

"I don't like this."

"I know. But like I said — I've got this. You have nothing to worry about."

As he walked away into the night, home to the type of family Georgie had always longed for, she only wished she could believe the same thing.

When she let herself back into her lodgings, her heart was beating so loudly that she wondered if Leo could hear the *rum-pum-pum*.

How embarrassing it would be if he could actually sense the fullness of her desire for him. He would think her a fool.

"Who is he?" Leo asked with a scowl as she shut the door behind her. He had moved to the sofa, and while she knew he would never admit it, she had an inkling that the head injury was bothering him more than he would ever admit.

"He's the physician," she said, confused at the question.

"I mean, who is he to you?"

His stare must be so perturbed because he didn't want anyone knowing of his existence.

"He is my friend," she answered softly, "and your secret is safe with him. I've told him that we will pay him once... once we are able to."

He nodded, apparently understanding just what she meant by that. Once he remembered who he was and had access to the wealth that must be awaiting him.

"Are you hungry?" she asked, and when he hesitated, she knew that must mean yes. "I'll prepare you something while I get your bath ready. I must apologize. I am not much of a cook, but I do have some bread and some stew that Carson's wife sent home."

"He's married, then."

"He is."

"And who is this Marshall you speak of?"

She busied herself collecting dishes and placing them down on the small counterspace where she made her simple meals.

"He's…"

"Not your husband."

She turned and looked at him over her shoulder, a coil of hair loosening from its pin as she did so. Without giving it much thought, she shoved the pin back in.

He wore a wry smile as he looked at her knowingly.

"No," she said and sighed at his understanding. "Not my husband."

"Why did you lie?"

"I never lied," she said, turning back away from the intensity of his stare, not wishing to be trapped by it any longer. Goodness, she wished she had made sure he was wearing a shirt. She must remedy that immediately. "You made an assumption."

"Who was here earlier, then?"

"Here? Marshall helped bring you here."

"I see."

She ladled the warmed stew Nan had sent into a bowl, running her finger over the chip in the edge of it that couldn't be helped before passing it to Leo. He accepted it with thanks, and she watched him as he carefully took the spoon, filling it with a small portion before lifting it to his lips and sipping thoughtfully. Definitely noble.

"How did you come to be on the docks?" he asked her, accepting the new glass of whiskey she passed him now. He was obviously using it to self-medicate from the pain, but it seemed to be working as his eyes had lost that pinched look he had been wearing since he arrived.

"It was my job to be there."

"You work on the docks?" His eyes narrowed, and she realized what he was thinking as she poured the first pot of boiled water into the small tub she had pulled from her bedroom.

"I am sometimes called to the docks, though not often, for they are usually overseen by the Thames Police," she corrected him. "We were called there after you were discovered. I work with Bow Street."

"Bow Street..." he murmured, looking down at his fingers, which were drumming a pattern on the table, one she recognized but couldn't quite place.

"I'm a detective," she said softly. "I'm not well-known, but that seems to work for us."

"A detective?" he asked incredulously, and the carefully crafted defenses that arose every time someone new discovered her profession locked themselves in place.

"Yes," she answered curtly. "A detective. And a good one at that."

"I never imagined you wouldn't be," he mused, leaning back to study her. "How did that come to be?"

"I—" She snapped her mouth shut. Why was she spilling all of her life's secrets to this man who was likely going to leave the moment he remembered who he was, which almost certainly included the fact that he should be living two neighborhoods away, on a street that was not so far in distance but as far as could be in status?

Because she couldn't help the draw to him, this inexplicable attraction that she had no right to feel.

"I think we should save that story for another day," she

said firmly, picking up his empty bowl and carrying it over to the wash stand.

"Let me help you with that," he said, placing his hands on the table to stand, and she shook her head.

"You need to rest. Besides, I'm sure you wouldn't know how anyway."

He paused for a moment, and she smirked, knowing she was right.

"Your bath is ready. It isn't much, I'm afraid, but it should clean away the Thames if nothing else. While you were sleeping, Marshall brought a new shirt and trousers for you. They're over by the fire. I'm going to retire for the night. If you need anything, I'll be through there," she said, nodding toward her bedroom. "Just knock. And please don't fall and drown yourself."

"Very well," he said, and, her clean up complete, she drew her hands together and began her retreat to her room.

"Georgie?"

"Yes?" she stopped.

"Thank you."

She nodded and continued on, shutting the door firmly behind her.

THE WOMAN HAD no idea what she was doing to him.

And he intended to keep it that way.

Leo couldn't explain this pull to her, but he thought she must have bewitched him, so intoxicated he was by her. He knew he had drank his fair share of whisky, but it wasn't the alcohol which had caused his blood to thrum within his veins.

It was her.

He removed his foul-smelling trousers, throwing them to

the side as he stepped into the tub she had prepared for him. She had been right — the tub was far too small and he had to sit like a child with his knees in toward his chest, but the hot water did help soothe his aching muscles.

He leaned his head back, closing his eyes, but her face appeared behind the shut lids anyway.

He couldn't say what it was about her that so drew him. She was no beauty, and yet she was striking. Her brown eyes were too wide, her nose too large, and two slightly crooked teeth stood out when she smiled.

But somehow together, the package was one that was more enticing than any other he could ever have imagined. At least, as far as he knew.

If he felt he was free to do so, he might very well knock on that bedroom door and see if she was as interested as he was. But he couldn't. It wouldn't be fair. Not to her, nor to whomever he might have left behind.

He would leave if he could, to rid himself of the temptation that was pulling at him, but at this point in time, he had nowhere else to go.

And, truthfully? He didn't know if he had it within him to leave. For then he just might never see her again.

CHAPTER 5

*T*he next morning, Leo sat up in startled alertness, heart pounding and breathing rapid. As he studied his surroundings, he felt even more confusion than he had gone to bed with. He blinked rapidly as he tried to remember just where he was and what he was doing here.

Then it all came rushing back — the last day, anyway.

He glanced to the empty hearth, but instead of shivering, he was filled with a warmth of home. As his gaze continued to take in the room, his heartbeat steadied and his breathing slowed. Tension released its hold on his shoulders and neck, and he released a sigh. He was here. He was with Georgie. He would be all right.

He touched the medal lying against his chest and turned it over, rubbing its surface with his fingers, marvelling at it. It was clearly well-crafted, with small gemstones inlaid into the silver. Who had made it for him, and why did he wear it?

He scrubbed a hand over his face as the nightmares came flooding back. A shout, a flash, a crack, and then — blackness.

Despite the sheen of sweat left on his skin as the panic

overtook him once more, the truth was that he would actually welcome the nightmares if they told him anything about who he was and what had happened.

But no. They were just enough to warn him away — but from what, he had no idea.

He struggled to his feet, walking over to the wash basin in the corner of the room, where he splashed cold water on his face to try to wake up. He looked around the small space to see if Georgie had already awoken, but there were no signs of her. Out the small window, the street before him was already awake, people going about their morning business in what was clearly an area of commerce.

He wished he could go out and find breakfast for the two of them — to do *something* to show Georgie some appreciation — but he didn't even have any coin to use.

Leo paced for a few minutes, impatient, needing to do something — *anything* — rather than just sit there. He had sat long enough, and despite his impatience, he was pleased that he was not nearly as weak as he had been just the day before.

A good sleep, that was all he had needed, he thought, just before a wave of dizziness threatened to bring him to the ground.

He placed a hand on the table, knowing he couldn't go out alone, and yet he also couldn't just sit here doing nothing.

He looked toward Georgie's door. He should leave her be. He really should. And yet...

His feet had a mind of their own as they hesitantly took steps toward the door. He knocked lightly, not wanting to wake her, and then louder as a sliver of worry overtook him. What if something had happened to her? What if, whoever was coming for him had determined his whereabouts and taken revenge on Georgie instead, who had done nothing but responded to his plea for help? What if—

Before he could think of it anymore, he took the door-knob within his hand and surged forward—before halting and standing completely still.

She was turned to the side, the mirror in front of her. Her eyes were cast down at the clothing beside her as she seemed to be selecting just what she should wear, her hair out of its pins and cascading around her in a waterfall of loose curls. He swallowed hard at the sight of her in only a thin chemise which did nothing to hide what was underneath.

He could see every sculpted line of her, from the protrusion of rosy nipples to the curve of her bottom.

And he liked what he saw.

She had all of the softness of a woman, her curves inviting him forward, and yet the planes of her body held such strength — her bottom firm and lifted, her shoulders wide and sculpted, her belly flat.

A bolt of desire surged through Leo with such strength that he couldn't imagine ever in his life wanting anything more.

Which was exactly the problem — in addition to the fact that he had let himself in uninvited, that she would think him a louse if she knew he was watching her like this, like some kind of rotter.

He recoiled in disgust with himself, wondering what type of reprobate he really was. He lifted a hand, thinking to shield his eyes from her, as he didn't think he could other-wise look away — at the same moment that she turned around.

Her eyes met his in a moment of shock, yes, but also… pain and remorse flashed through them, and she quickly swiveled around, hiding herself with a garment she picked up from before her.

"I—I'm sorry," he stuttered as he backed away, knowing he was likely just making the situation worse, but unable to simply leave her. "I shouldn't have—that is, I was worried when you didn't answer my knock, and I—"

"Just go," she said, her voice muffled by the shirt she was pulling over her head, her back muscles flexing powerfully with the effort.

He was captivated, rooted to the spot, but as the generous brown curls began to poke through the hole of the shirt, he turned and did something he hoped he didn't have reason to do often — he ran.

GEORGIE WASN'T one who took much time to prepare herself. She wore simple clothes, made for moving efficiently. London's criminals did not care how made up her face was — for the most part — so she added no rouge nor charcoal.

Even her hair was typically fashioned in a simple braid that she then coiled and pinned to keep it out of the way.

But today she took much longer. Not because she was taking extra time to improve her looks — goodness but she could never let Leopold think such a thing — but because she needed a moment to steady herself after, well, whatever that was.

She held her head high when she finally walked out of her room, finding Leo sitting uncomfortably at the kitchen table.

"Listen, Georgie, I'm sorry, I—"

She waved his apology away.

"You don't need to apologize for your opinion of what you saw."

"But that's the thing. I—"

"You saw me nearly undressed and you were repulsed. I understand. Most men would be. I have the shoulders of a laborer, my friend's mother used to tell me. 'Don't use them anymore,' she'd say, 'or they shall only grow, and no man ever wants a woman who is stronger than him.' I understand. I do not look like a woman. I'm not exactly a diamond of the sea, or whatever you lot call the women you are so enamored with, but I did not invite you into my bedroom to pass judgement."

She stopped, hearing how rapidly she was breathing, and turned from him as she began to make coffee in the small corner of the room, trying to cover her shame which, she told herself, she had no right to feel.

"Georgie. Would you stop talking and let me speak?"

"I don't want to hear it," she said, refusing to turn around, too embarrassed at the moment to meet his eyes. When she had looked up to find him standing there, watching her, not only were his eyes filled with disgust, but he had stepped back with a grimace on his face, his hand lifted to shield her from his delicate vision. "Next time you don't like something you see, simply turn around and walk away," she finished, turning around now and placing his coffee in front of him with such a thump that it spilled over the edges and made a puddle on the table.

"Bloody hell," she cursed as she went to find a cloth to clean the rest of it.

"Impressive," he remarked, and when she finally lifted her gaze to him, he gestured toward her. "Your cursing."

"Ah, yes," she said, snapping up the rag and lifting her own coffee to her lips. She had never been much of a tea drinker. "Another all-too-masculine aspect of my countenance."

"Will you shut up, woman, and let me speak?"

She choked on her coffee, spitting it out at the bluntness of his words, and he rose, patting her on the back to help her get it out.

"You all right now?"

"Fine," she croaked.

"Well, the good thing is you can hardly speak now, anyway, so *I* finally have the chance to do so."

She glared at him.

"First, I didn't mean to enter your rooms uninvited. I did knock, but you didn't answer."

She had been too busy humming to herself, for she had been enjoying the companionship. More embarrassment.

"I was worried that something had happened to you — that I might have invited trouble to your house. I had to make sure you were all right."

She paused, determining that his words did have some truth to them, and it somewhat warmed her to think that there was a man who cared enough to look after her wellbeing. But that still didn't excuse the way he had reacted to her.

He looked down for a moment, clearing his throat before continuing.

"My reaction… it was not directed at you."

She raised her eyebrows in disbelief.

"I was disgusted with *myself*… for staring at you when I had no right to do so, and for… for liking it."

"You liked it." Her tone was laced with disbelief. No man had ever before told her that he liked looking at her frame. Not that she had much occasion to ask what one thought.

The truth was, most men of Georgie's acquaintance were her friends. Men liked Georgie well enough — in fact, many of them liked her even better than their own wives. But they liked her as well as they would any other gentleman. They treated her as one of them, not as a member of what was supposed to be the fairer sex.

She didn't blame them. It was just as much her own fault, for the way she dressed, the way she carried herself, and for her profession. But she had realized early on how men saw her, and had eventually decided that instead of fighting the role she had been provided, she would embrace it.

It was Leo's turn to clear his throat and seem slightly uncomfortable, as he looked from one side to the next before meeting her eyes.

"I did."

She nodded. She appreciated the apology and the attempt at mollifying her, but she wasn't about to be swayed by fancy words.

"You don't believe me," he said, crossing his arms over his chest and looking deeper into her eyes. She looked away. They were too probing, saw too much. She was the one who was supposed to determine more about others. No one was supposed to come too close to her.

"It doesn't matter," she said, attempting to turn away, but he caught her by the shoulders and held her tight.

"You told me that you can always tell when people are lying."

"I can."

"Well then, overcome your own self-doubt and *look* at me. You'll know I am telling the truth."

She wanted to stomp her foot and tell him to let her go, that she didn't need to face the reality of it once more, but she was also aware that he wasn't going to let this go until she did as he bid. She finally sighed, turning around to stare him in the face.

And was shocked to find that he was telling the truth.

CHAPTER 6

*S*he didn't walk like a lady.

She walked quickly, purposefully, like a woman on a mission — which he supposed she was. Waves of dizziness threatened to overcome him, but Leo was determined that he was not going to succumb nor show any signs of weakness in front of her. She had seen enough of that from him already. Best not to make it a habit.

"Do many people know that Bow Street has women detectives?" he asked, keeping pace even as beads of sweat broke out on his brow.

"There is just one female detective. And no, not many are aware," she said, shaking her head. "It's best to be kept that way."

She turned to him with a look of intention, and he nodded in understanding. His concentration was currently split between putting one foot in front of the other without falling over and also preventing himself from staring.

When Georgie had emerged from her bedroom this morning, he had come to the startling realization of just why he had, in his initial haze, assumed that there was a gentleman in the house.

It was Georgie herself.

She was dressed this morning in a linen shirt and breeches that hugged the entire line of her leg in a nearly indecent way. He had swallowed when she turned around. Now, walking just a step behind her... it was agonizing. Beneath her worn but well-fitted black jacket, which was slightly too well tailored to ever suit a man, she wore a navy waistcoat. A black top hat was pulled down low over her coil of hair, but enough peaked out the bottom to tell anyone who wondered that she was most definitely female.

Not that it wasn't apparent by looking at the back of her.

"Where are we going?"

She turned her head to look at him, and he guessed he must not have looked the vision of health, for she came to a sudden stop.

"Are you all right?"

"Fine."

"Are you sure? Perhaps this is too much, too soon. We can go back."

"I'm fine. Where are we going?"

"The docks," she said, turning back around and continuing, although slower this time. "I'd like to return to where we found you, see if anything strikes your memory or if, perhaps, anyone else might recognize you."

"I was found in the water. Have you heard any more about the explosion?"

"I have," she nodded. "There was a vessel just outside the mouth of the Thames that was carrying gunpowder. It met with an unexpected explosion. It was, apparently, an accident, but we find it suspicious that it would happen so close to London, with you onboard. For now, I want you to try to remember anything you can about the ship and how you ended up where we found you. At the time, you were not in your senses. We need to determine why you were at sea in the first place."

She stopped suddenly in the middle of Thames Street, turning on her heel so quickly that he nearly ran into her. He had to reach out and grasp her arms to keep from knocking her over.

He allowed his hands to remain upon her for a few seconds longer than necessary, until she looked down at his grip with a raised eyebrow and he finally let her go.

She took a breath, as though trying to remember just why she had stopped, and he could see when memory returned.

"Leopold," she said, her brown eyes searching from one of his to the other, "here's the truth. I honestly don't know if you are ever going to regain any of your memories. I don't know much of such things, but Carson said it's just as likely that you will remain in the dark for the rest of your life as it is that you will recall your past. However, I promise you that I *will* help you discover who you are. The most likely way for me to do that is to continue my own investigation as to what your identity might be, and then return you to wherever — or *whom*ever — you belong."

He attempted a smile to cover the panic at her words at the thought that he might never regain all that he had lost. "I'm not a lost puppy," he said, arching an eyebrow.

"No," she shook her head, "you are far too disagreeable for a puppy."

With that, she turned and resumed her quick stride, and he took a deep breath as he had to run to catch up. She was taller than most women, he mused as he watched her from behind, but he was a big man, and her head reached just above his shoulder. The perfect height to kiss her, he mused, but he knew to say such a thing aloud would only capture more of her ire. For whatever reason, she thought that he was mocking her when he said anything regarding his attraction to her, but the truth was, he was not in a place to offer her anything more than friendship.

Not until he knew what circumstances awaited him — which meant that it was best to continue along with her little investigation until it came to a satisfactory conclusion.

"We're here," she said, as they arrived, the smell of the Thames welcoming them along with the cacophony of noise. The fishermen had just returned with their morning catches, and the dockworkers were unloading early arrivals, shouting to one another as they worked their line of deliveries.

Georgie stopped, staring down the long line of ships, and while Leo was overwhelmed at just where to begin, Georgie seemed to be used to such chaos. "This way," she said. "Let's start at the beginning of the dock and work our way down. You can see if anything resounds with you, and we will also determine whether anyone recognizes you."

It didn't seem that he had any choice but to follow her, which he did, although his head began to ache something fierce at the overwhelming of his senses.

"How are we going to recognize anyone or anything in this mob?" he asked, but even as he voiced the question, he heard Georgie's name being called out, and he turned along with her.

"Georgie!" It was a young man, who looked hardly twenty, but dressed fine enough, clearly a man of merchant status. "I've been looking for you," he said, nearly out of breath as he caught up with her.

"Benson," she exclaimed with a wide grin that caused a twist of Leo's stomach akin to jealousy, "It's been some time!"

Then she stepped in with a quick embrace that nearly earned a growl from Leo's throat, one he had to swallow down with much astonishment. He had no hold over Georgie, so why was he acting like a jealous lover? Once he discovered his identity, he'd be gone — he was sure of it. Perhaps it was just that he wished *this* woman — the laughing, jovial, friendly one with everyone else — would treat him in such a way rather than with the disdain she seemed to regard him.

"I've news," Benson said, before looking over at Leo with question.

Georgie looked over at him with apology. "A moment, if you don't mind?"

He nodded, and she and the man stepped away. They didn't move far, however, and Leo captured snippets of their conversation. After a few minutes of discussion to which Georgie seemed increasingly concerned, she nodded, thanked the man, and then Benson left her as they continued on.

"What was that about?" he couldn't help but ask, and she eyed him as though wondering whether or not to trust him.

"There have been rumors for some time now. About a potential change to the criminal system," she finally said, although she looked back and forth as though questioning whether anyone might be listening.

"Oh? In what regard?"

"In terms of punishment. That sentences should be more severe, to further discourage crime." She rubbed a hand against her forehead.

"Is that a bad thing?" he asked, frowning, not understanding her concern.

"I suppose it depends who you are," she said sarcastically, and he placed his hands on his hips as he stared at her in exasperation.

"You're going to have to tell me exactly what you mean by that."

"I mean that currently punishments don't fit the particular crimes. They fit the stations in life. A woman without any connections, any funds to save herself, any ability to earn a living, steals in order to feed her child? Life in an institution after she is declared insane due to hysteria. A nobleman murders a vagrant? Nothing. He continues living his life."

Leo sighed. He could understand her vexation, and yet he wondered just what she had to do with all of it.

"It is how it is, though, is it not, Georgie? What is anyone supposed to do about it? I know a nobleman may receive more freedoms, but he also has many more responsibilities, does he not?"

She snorted. "It's such a coincidence, isn't it, that those are the men who make the laws in the first place?" She shook her head. "If they're not going to make it any better, it's best to be left as it is. I'm doing what I can to determine who is behind this motion, and will hopefully convince him to leave it alone."

The idea didn't sit well with him. Despite Georgie's insistence that he was of the upper class, he had no idea where he resided on the ladder of life's stations. However, he knew she had a point about the differing rights provided each class. If she went up against a man with more power than she expected, she would be in trouble.

"I hope you're being careful."

She eyed him. "I'm always careful. And I don't need anyone to watch over me."

He nodded, realizing that this was not the right tactic to take with Georgie.

"Does anything look familiar to you?" Georgie asked, eyeing him as she changed the subject.

He crossed his arms over his chest as he looked around. "No. Nor do I feel comfortable here, which tells me this is not likely a place that I often frequented."

"Very well," she said with a sigh, pulling a pocket watch out of her jacket, consulting it. "I'm late, as it is."

"Are you returning to Bow Street?"

"No." She shook her head. "I've... friends to meet."

Leo fought the urge to know just who she was meeting with, wondering more about her personal life but knowing that it was not exactly his place to question it. "Very well."

"I'll walk home with you and then will continue on."

Why did home — with her — sound so inviting? "I don't need a nursemaid. I can return to your rooms by myself."

She narrowed her eyes. "I'm not sure I feel comfortable with that. You might not remember where you are going, or could become lost or dizzy, and then what would you do? You would be—"

"Georgie," he interrupted her, ensuring that there was no room for argument in his tone. "You don't need looking after? Well, neither do I. Point me in the right direction, and I'll be fine."

She looked conflicted for a moment before she finally relented, walking with him to New Queen Street before pointing him the way he was to go. "This way," she said. "I'll be back within a couple of hours."

"Georgie?" he said as she turned to go.

"Yes?"

"Enjoy yourself," he said, wishing for more, but knowing that it was the most he could say, for now.

She nodded, her expression guarded, before turning and walking away.

CHAPTER 7

*G*eorgie knew her friends would be able to ascertain her distraction, but she couldn't simply *not* meet them. Then they would know for certain something had come up. So instead, she pasted on a smile and sat down to tea — or coffee, in her case — with them in the small tea shop.

She felt like livestock in the middle of the dainty room with its soft pink, blue, and yellow walls covered in pale watercolors, but it was one of Alice's favorites, and the sweetness of the biscuits the shop baked was enough to entice her to agree to the location.

Fortunately, today all of the attention was upon Rose, who had found happiness with her love, Lord Perry Belmont.

"Tell us more about the wedding," Alice said dreamily. "It shall be fun to return to Lyme Regis."

Rose nodded with a smile that told them just how much she was looking forward to returning home, as well as the place where she and Perry would make their residence, at least until the time when he would have to take on his duties as the Earl of Sheriden.

"It will be a rather small wedding, which is what the two of us are quite pleased about," she said. "Perry's mother would have loved a grand wedding, as she likely would have with his brother, but since his death, they have gradually come to accept that while he is now Lord Richmond, Perry is still his own man and will make his own decisions."

"Quite forward thinking of them," Alice mused, more familiar with society as the sister of a baron with a marquess for a brother-in-law.

"It is, actually," Rose said, tilting her head to the side, a small smile playing around her lips as she considered her situation. "I honestly never would have thought to be accepted by them, but they seem to be fine with whatever — and whomever — Perry chooses."

Georgie smiled as she encircled the coffee cup with both hands, staring down into its depths. She was thrilled for all three of her friends and the love matches they had made, but she had to admit there were moments — usually when she was home, alone, with no one but the fire for company — that she wished she would one day have the opportunity to find someone for herself.

Someone like Leo, she mused, although first she had to determine if that would ever even be an option.

"I saw Lady Anne the other day," Madeline said. She was a slight, blond woman whose appearance might fool most into thinking that she was weak, as Georgie had first assumed upon becoming acquainted with her the previous year through her colleague, Drake. Madeline, however, had shown more strength than anyone Georgie had ever met when her life had been in danger.

Drake and Madeline were now married, and Georgie couldn't imagine a more well-suited pair.

"How is she?" Rose asked gently. Lady Anne Fitzgerald was supposed to have married Perry's brother and, upon his death, the two families had assumed that she would wed Perry instead. All of that had changed upon Perry meeting Rose.

"She's actually doing quite well," Madeline said. "You recall the day on Rotten Row when the horses of Perry's curricle nearly ran away with her?"

"How could I ever forget?" Rose asked wryly, and Madeline nodded in understanding.

"Yes, well, when Clark rescued her that day, it seems it was not the last the two of them saw of one another. They have spent a great deal of time together since that fateful day."

"What does her family think of a merchant courting their daughter?" Alice asked with wide eyes. Clark worked with Madeline, and while he was partnering with her in the stone business, it was hard to imagine how it would ever be good enough for a nobleman's daughter.

"I'm not sure they actually know of the match yet," Madeline said with a slight wince.

"Well, I'm glad to know that she has found love again," Rose said softly. "She seemed to have been so in love with Perry's brother. And Clark's rescue was rather romantic."

"Even though you missed most of it as you were busy rescuing Perry at the time." Alice laughed.

"Even though," Rose agreed.

They were silent for a moment until Alice turned her shrewd gaze on Georgie. "You're awfully quiet today."

"Me?" Georgie asked with a swallow, knowing that nothing was ever going to get by Alice. "I'm just enjoying listening to the three of you."

Alice quirked an eyebrow. "You expect us to believe that you don't have an opinion to share?"

"I'm glad that Lady Anne is happy," Georgie said truthfully. "And of course, I can hardly wait for your wedding,

Rose. I am also looking forward to visiting Lyme Regis again. It is rather... peaceful there."

"It is, isn't it?" Alice said with a beaming smile. "Well, tell us Georgie, are there any new and interesting cases that you have been investigating these days?"

"Oh, nothing of much importance," she said breezily. She had no idea why she didn't tell them about Leo. She normally did entrust them with any of her cases that were not confidential, but as much as she knew she should ask them for help with his identity, a small part of her wanted to keep him to herself. Besides, she knew that if she began to speak of Leo, these women, who had become closer to her than anyone else in London besides Marshall, would likely see right through her telling and ascertain her feelings toward him.

Feelings that she couldn't entirely identify herself yet.

Best to keep it all to herself. At least for now.

"There's a case of... misplaced identity that I am looking into, but that's all I can say," she said cryptically, not wanting to lie to them.

"How interesting," Alice said, looking at Georgie with assessing eyes over the top of her teacup. "Well, when you can say more, you know we always love to hear a good story."

"I know," Georgie said, placing her empty coffee cup back down upon the table. "Well, ladies, it has been an interesting hour as always, but I best go. I must stop at Bow Street before continuing on."

"Well, we will be seeing much of you soon," Alice said as she stood, "for we will all be leaving for Lyme in two weeks' time. You are going to travel with us, are you not?"

"Two weeks?" Georgie repeated. She had lost all track of time. She was looking forward to Rose's wedding, but had forgotten how soon it was. What was she going to do with

Leopold? "Yes," she said, noting their questioning gazes. "Two weeks. I would love to accompany you."

Unless she had an extra guest along with her. How much could possibly change in a couple of weeks?

* * *

LEO SWORE as he burned his finger on the pot when he tried to pick it up out of the fire.

He should have known better. But how in all that was holy did one do such a thing?

He rubbed his temple as he looked around the small room. It was still welcoming. It was still comfortably decorated. But it was no longer orderly. And it was no longer looking like Georgie had just left.

The truth was, if she came home and didn't find him here, she would probably think that a pack of thieves had broken in and ransacked every cupboard, every drawer.

But no. It had just been him.

He *was* rather proud of the result of it all. He just had no idea what her reaction was going to be.

He was going to find out now, as he heard the door scrape open.

"Leo? I—"

She stood, framed in the doorway with the setting sun silhouetting her frame. She reminded him of a sun goddess. A horrified sun goddess.

"What—what happened here?"

"I cooked you dinner."

"You—what?"

That stare turned to him now, caught between astonishment and terror.

"You've been doing a great deal for me, so I wanted to return the favor. To do so, I thought I would cook dinner for you. Only… it seems that I likely have never cooked dinner before. I asked for advice from the woman in the market-place, and while she initially had a good chuckle over it, she did eventually provide some directions. I found some coin in your drawer, but I will pay you back as soon as I am able to, I promise…"

He stopped, realizing he was prattling on for no good reason.

"Anyway. Here you go."

He lifted the plate toward her, now filled with a generous portion of rather burned chicken, potatoes and vegetables that he wasn't sure he could properly name.

"I—thank you."

He stared at her for a moment as he realized that one of her eyes was… wet. Was she—no, she couldn't be. Not Georgie.

"Are you crying?"

"No."

"I know I made a mess, but I will clean it. I promise. I just didn't know where anything was or what to do."

He threw his hands up at his side, and then she sniffed. Damn it. His stomach twisted. He had done the wrong thing. He should have known. This hadn't felt comfort-able, hadn't seemed to be something he would ever do, but he hadn't been able to sit still and, despite his assur-ance otherwise, had no idea just where in London he should go to try to work on the unravelling of his own mystery.

So he had tried to cook dinner.

"I'm not crying," she said resolutely, her chin set as she stepped into the room. "I don't cry."

"No?"

Hope sprang in his chest. Maybe she had come down with an illness of some sort. Not that he would wish that upon her. Bollocks, he had no idea what he wanted at the moment.

"I just... no one but my mother has ever cooked for me before. At least, not that I can remember. And I really, really hate to cook. So to come home and not have to think about what to prepare, well..." She shrugged. "Perhaps I am slightly overcome. It's been a day."

"So... would you like to come eat?"

She nodded. "I would."

She took off her jacket, resting it over the back of the chair, and the moment of comfort between them, the fact that she felt at ease enough with him to sit in a shirt and waistcoat warmed him inside.

She didn't look at him as she took a bite. Then another. Soon she was digging in with enthusiasm that filled him with an immeasurable amount of pride.

"What do you think?" he finally couldn't help but ask.

"It's actually very, very good," she said, looking up at him with a grin. "Well done."

Well, this was much better than her tears. "Good," he said smugly. "I'm glad."

They ate for a moment in companionable silence, and he watched her, content in knowing that he had been the one to feed her, that he had looked after her in some small, though insignificant, way.

"Why do you wear men's clothing?"

His next breath stalled in his chest. He hadn't meant to ask it out loud. The question had been pestering him all day, however, and it seemed that he was a man who would always say what was on his mind.

Her brown eyes flew up to meet his as her fork clattered against the cracked plate. She paused for a moment, assessing him as though trying to determine just why he was asking such a question.

"Sometimes in my work, I find myself in situations where I have to be quick on my feet, move my body in ways that can be restricted by skirts," she said. "Men's clothing is much more practical for such a thing."

He nodded. "I see. But you wear women's clothing as well?"

"I wear what makes the most sense for the activity of the day," she said, not without a touch of defensiveness. "And besides…"

"Yes?"

"It's not just the clothing that is more freeing. It's also what a man is able to do. I like to be able to do as I please, and to, I don't know, confuse people. Sometimes I wish I had been born a man."

She must have read the shock in his gaze.

"Not like that, although I know some women truly do believe they were meant to be men and choose to live that way. What I mean, I suppose, is that if women were afforded the same freedoms and opportunities as men, then we would be able to do more, be taken more seriously, and not be questioned for every bit of independence we require. Does that make sense?"

He picked up a piece of bread and stared at her as he chewed. "I suppose, when you put it that way, it does."

She nodded. "I know most people think I'm half-mad. Especially—" she shook her head, not finishing her thought, and he couldn't help but see a fleeting expression of pain cross her face. She shrugged. "I find that I don't particularly care what they think."

"You must be followed around by half the men in London with your breeches hugging your bottom like that."

"Are you mocking me again?" She stared at him with eyes narrowed in chagrin, and he sighed impatiently as he shook his head.

"Not at all. Why do you have such trouble believing in what I am saying?"

"Because," she said softly, looking down at her plate, "no one has ever said such things to me before."

Then they must be fools, all, every man who would ever believe her to be anyone but a woman deserving of such praise. However, he was smugly glad of it, for it provided him the opportunity to be the first.

"Tell me, how did you come to work as a detective?"

"You don't approve, do you?"

"I never said that. Don't make assumptions."

"Very well," she said with a curt nod. "I'm sorry."

"So..."

She shrugged, standing and taking her plate over to the countertop. "I never knew my father."

A sad story, then, although not completely shocking as it was far too common.

"Go on."

"My mother was both mother and father to me. Between the two of us, we could take on anything. She did her best, working as a seamstress, but as she aged, her eyes did with her, and she had trouble completing the work. Soon enough, she could hardly see or work anymore. I did what I could, ran around the streets, making an honest living sending messages, holding horses for men, usually pretending I was a boy to do so."

His heart ached at the thought of her, so young and forced to carry out such work. Except he knew this story was going to get worse. "And then?"

"We couldn't make enough to live off. My mother... she stole."

"Stole what?"

"Food. Bread. Linens." Her words were soft, nearly whispered. Her hands were in fists, placed on the counter in front of her. "The first offence, she was sentenced to two weeks in a house of correction. The second, a month. But then…" her voice cracked, "she knew I was alone, had no idea what had happened to me nor who would look after me. The first time she was imprisoned, I had to fend for myself for two weeks. The second, a month. I was ten years old. She spent her nights wailing, until they all believed her to be mad. Eventually, they decided that she was."

She turned completely away from him now, her voice but an echo around the room.

"They moved her to Bedlam. She's still there."

$\mathcal{W}$hy had she told him such things? She squeezed her eyes shut, in the hopes that, by not looking at him, he might be gone, and she would not appear to be the fool she felt.

She was wrong, of course.

When she opened them, he was standing in front of her instead, his strong, warm hands gently wrapping around her arms.

"That's ridiculous. She was only trying to feed her family and look after her daughter."

Georgie nodded jerkily.

"Well, it was why I became a detective. I want to find justice, but where it's merited. When it comes to such petty crimes… I determine for myself what is warranted to be punished."

He frowned, and she waited for him to question why she would feel that was up to her to do so. Fortunately, he did no such thing.

"So that is why you are so intent on ensuring that reforms

aren't enacted to push for harsher punishments," he murmured, and she nodded jerkily.

"It's not only my mother," she said. "There are so many people who are just like her. People who just want to feed their families, but have lost everything, for one reason or another. I can respect a merchant who makes a good life for himself, who builds wealth through his hard work, but sometimes it just irks me that a person might receive such preferential treatment based on the family he or she was born into."

He frowned as he looked down at her. "You must be careful. That sounds an awful lot like anarchy."

"And you sound an awful lot like the upper crust from where I am sure you come."

Her breathing was harsh now, her heartbeat rapid at both his nearness and her passion for their subject of conversation. He said he understood, but she wondered whether or not he was just placating her. She was sure it was never something he would have to overly worry about, and she was caught up for a moment with a new thought.

"Would you come with me tomorrow, if I told you I wanted to show you something?"

"Of course," he said, surprising her with his lack of hesitation when he didn't even know what she was suggesting. "Where do you want to go?"

"It's a surprise," she said, wondering if he would refuse if she told him what she was planning. "And then..." she began and took a breath before adding, "I had another thought."

"Oh?"

"Alice says there is to be a party tomorrow night. It will be held at her sister-in-law's parents' home. It's quite the event, and even I have been before. The Keswicks are wealthy merchants and always invite a healthy mix of people to the yearly party. I was thinking we should attend."

"We should?"

"Yes," she said resolutely. "This year is a masquerade, so we could attend anonymously. There is less chance you would be in danger as no one is likely to recognize you if you keep to the shadows, and you would be free to walk around and see if anything or anyone stirs your memory. If you truly felt comfortable, we could introduce you to a few people who I know we can trust."

"You trust people within the nobility?"

She nodded. "I might not like the preferential treatment the nobility receive, but I am not so hard-headed that I can't see there are still good people who possess titles. My friend Alice is married to the brother of a marquess, and she has many connections who have proven to be trustworthy in previous situations. I would trust them. Madeline and Drake will also be there. Drake is another detective."

"Is he now."

Was that jealously lacing his voice? No. It couldn't be. She quirked an eyebrow at him. "He is married to my friend, although I have known him for some time. He is one of my closest friends."

"I see."

"What do you think? Would you attend?"

"With you on my arm, how could I refuse?"

She rolled her eyes at him as she began to turn away, but he reached out and caught her arm within his hand, slowly turning her around to face him.

"Georgie," he said, his voice just above a whisper. "Why do you continue to rebuke me?"

"What do you mean?" she asked, hearing her own breathlessness.

"How many times do I have to tell you how attractive, how appealing you are, for you to believe me?"

"I just... I know you don't remember who you are, but no

matter where you come from, I'm sure you have no shortage of women who are interested in you. I can't see how I would have anything to attract you, when I do for no one else."

He stared at her for a moment, his eyes so intense that she couldn't help but shiver. She was being honest with him — she always was — and she couldn't see why he would lie to her.

But how could he be telling the truth?

She didn't have any longer to think about it, however, as he leaned down and took her lips with his.

Georgie stood still for a moment, stunned, unmoving as she took a moment to determine whether this was really happening.

He kissed as wondrously as she would have ever predicted, and after a couple of moments, she stopped thinking altogether as she allowed herself to become caught up in all he was offering her.

Standing this close, he smelled divine. Somehow the scent of her lavender soap was completely different when it was upon his skin. He tasted like wine and cinnamon and desire.

Desire for her?

Her body went nearly limp in his arms, and he responded only by tightening his grip around her. Until his tongue touched the seam of her lips and then her body was spurred to life, pressing closer against him as she locked her arms around his neck and gave just as good as he, her lips furiously moving over his as his tongue swept into her mouth, his motions as purposeful and determined as anything else he ever seemed to do.

His large hand spanned the back of her head, holding her in place, and for the first time in her life, Georgie was overwhelmed by someone else's strength. How good it felt for a man to hold her in his arms as a woman he had full intentions of coming to know even better. He spread fire through every one of her limbs, and she began to burn for him deep within, in ways she would never have thought possible.

Then, just as fiercely as he had taken her lips, he released her, and she stepped back, nearly falling over at the shock of suddenly standing without his touch.

"I—what just—why did you—"

"Don't you ever again question the fact that you are a beautiful, intriguing woman who should be properly and regularly reminded of such a thing," he said ferociously, and she could only nod jerkily at his request. It was actually less of a request and more of a command, but she didn't seem to have any power within her to argue.

He turned away, running a hand through his hair, which was obviously a touch too long.

"I'm going to bed," he said, beginning to stride away, until he stopped awkwardly, realizing that his bed was, in fact, in the middle of the room where they currently stood and Georgie would have laughed if she wasn't so flummoxed.

"I suppose that means I'll be going," she said quietly, her entire body in such turmoil that she didn't mind leaving him to have a moment alone anyway. "Goodnight, Leo."

And then, feeling his eyes upon her with each footfall, she walked into her bedroom, her legs shaking every step of the way.

* * *

LEO WAS ALREADY WAITING for Georgie when she awoke the next morning.

The truth was, he had hardly been able to sleep. Every time he closed his eyes, he saw her. Every time his fingers touched the blanket, it was Georgie's skin he felt upon them. Every time he heard a noise, he imagined her tossing and turning in her bed, equally as bothered as he was.

He had kissed her to prove his point.

It had taken every bit of control to pull himself away from her before he took things any further.

At least it told him that he was likely a better man than he had originally thought. For if he was the reprobate he had first expected of himself, he would have spent the night with the woman in his arms.

"Good morning," she said, her voice infused with an obvious forced chipper. "Did you sleep well?"

"No."

Her hands stilled upon the kettle as she moved to place it over the fire at the conviction in his words. He heard it himself and he didn't care. "I'm sorry to hear that. I know that must not be the most comfortable place to sleep but—"

"Georgie."

He was beside her in moments, and she started to find him there next to her.

"I couldn't sleep because I couldn't stop thinking about you. About what it felt like to have you in my arms, your lips under mine. About how your body might respond should I ever have the opportunity to touch it, skin to skin."

He couldn't help himself from skimming his hands over her sides, around her waist, down her hips, then back up again.

"I went to bed because if I stayed in your presence another moment I would have said to hell with it and would have taken you right there on the kitchen table."

Her eyes, already wide and searching, blinked rapidly.

"You—you would have?"

"I would have."

"Would you still?"

"Would I still?" he scoffed. "I would take you at any moment, in any place, on any day." He paused. "If I could. But I cannot — and you deserve better than that."

She lowered her hands to interlace her fingers with his. "I —I hardly know what to say."

"I feel as though I am a man used to getting what I want," he grunted. "And I want you. Badly. But I can't move forward. Not until I know that I am free to do so."

"You're a man with honor."

"Apparently," he said, shaking his head. "Damn it all."

She laughed then, a loud, long laugh that he wanted to hear more of, that he knew he would miss with an intensity if he was ever without it. He prayed that when he discovered his identity, he would be a single man, one who was free to come back and court Georgie properly, to show her how special she was, how she deserved to have a man worship her as he most assuredly would.

She was wearing a dress today, a soft linen that was rather feminine, although it was in a dark green that still seemed appropriate for her. He picked up some of the fabric near her waist, rubbing it between his finger and thumb, as he assessed how worn it was. He wondered if she had attired herself in such feminine clothing for his own benefit — or if it was because he had told her how much he enjoyed her in breeches and she was just trying to spite him.

She looked down at his fingers, apparently correctly determining what he was thinking, for she jerked away hastily and began to ramble.

"I forgot to tell you yesterday — while we were out, a friend brought some more clothes for you."

"Another friend of the male persuasion?" he said wryly.

"No, actually," she said with a quick shake of her head as she poured coffee for both of them. "A female friend who happens to have some clothing on hand."

"Whatever for?"

She surprised him by turning a deep shade of red and

turning away. She cleared her throat before she managed to mutter, "costumes."

"Costumes? Is she in theatre?"

Georgie shook her head and Leo paused for a moment before understanding dawned.

"Oooh…" He laughed. "I see. Role play."

"Yes," she said, the words choked out of her, and then she whirled around, pushing a stray lock of hair off her forehead. She took a sip of coffee, but it must have been too hot for she spit it right back out into her cup.

"Are you all right?" he asked, hurrying over to her side.

"Just fine," she said, waving him away. "Here. There's some bread there too if you're hungry."

"Thank you," he said, helping himself. "Do you have any sugar?"

"I do," she said, passing it to him, the two of them moving together in the kitchen as though they had for years. She stopped, turning to look at him with wide eyes. "Is that how you like your coffee?"

He poured the spoonful into the cup and took a sip. "It is," he confirmed, a smile spreading across his lips at the realization. "How did I know that?"

"I'm not sure," she said, her own smile slightly saddened for some reason. "But hopefully that's good news."

"I hope so too," he said fervently. "Now. Just where are you taking me?"

CHAPTER 9

*W*hat the hell was wrong with her? Georgie was of a mind to smack *herself* across the face. She was behaving worse than an innocent debutante. Sure, she wasn't exactly widely experienced herself, though she had seen more in her lifetime than many women ever would.

But somehow, when the subjects she usually deftly maneuvered through arose in conversation with Leo, they took on an altogether different meaning.

She had barely been able to explain the origin of the clothing he had retreated into her bedroom to don, and just the thought of him changing was causing all sorts of fire to dance over her skin. Then, in trying to cover up how affected she was, she had burned her mouth, and had hardly managed to hide her upset that he had actually remembered something about his past. She should be celebrating the fact, but instead she was selfishly upset, for she knew the sooner he regained his memories, the sooner he would be gone, out of her life forever.

She was the only woman detective in London, and she had held her wits in the most dire of situations. Surely she could control herself around a man who didn't even have a memory.

"Come," she said once he had emerged from the room. She did her very best to ignore the fact that the breeches were not only a decade behind in fashion but also a smidge too tight, showing off the best of his lower-half assets. "You'll soon find out where we're off to. How do you feel about walking a bit less than a half hour?"

She crossed the room, lacing her fingers into his hair as she turned his head to assess his injury. He froze at her touch, likely worried that she was coming on to him again, but then relaxed when he realized what she was doing.

"Have you been cleaning this?" she demanded, noting the bits of blood still dried into his hair.

"I've tried."

"Come here," she said, taking a piece of linen and wetting it in the washbasin. She began to pass it over his hair, rushing so that she wouldn't have any time to notice how silky the strands were, or how perfect they felt between her fingers. She opened the jar of paste that Carson had left and dabbed a bit of it onto the wound.

"Ouch!" he exclaimed at her roughness, and she muttered an apology before she snapped the jar shut once more.

"Ready?" she asked him, and he nodded.

"Ready."

"Should we hire a hack?" she asked, looking at him a bit appraisingly.

Shaking his head, he assured, "I'm fine."

"Very well," she said, and then he followed her out the door as they began their journey through London.

Georgie was amused by how mesmerized Leo seemed to be as they walked and she tried to see their journey from the viewpoint of a man who wouldn't have spent any time walking — or even visiting — such an area. The farther they went, the more the streets changed from the bustle of merchants and shoppers in Cheapside to the slower pace of the impoverished and desperate of the neighborhoods they entered.

Instinctively, he stepped closer to Georgie, holding onto her elbow and pressing her close to his side. She looked over at him, one side of her lips curled.

"Nervous?" she asked lightly, and he shook his head as he looked intensely from side to side. "Not to worry, I'll protect you."

It took a moment for him to register what she said, and she couldn't help but laugh when he turned to her with an expression that was something between surprise and annoyance.

"I appreciate your concern, Leo, truly I do, but the truth is, I've been walking these streets since I took my first steps."

"Georgie!" A voice cried out, proving her point, coming from the doorway of a tavern on the corner.

"Hello, Fred!" she called back as they continued down the street, and she pulled Leo to one side to avoid a bucket of slops being poured from above.

"How do you know him?" Leo asked.

"Fred? He's owned that tavern for as long as I have been alive. He looks out for everyone. And if you are ever wondering what's happening in this neighborhood, he'll know, or at least, he'll know who you should ask."

"And just which neighborhood are we in?"

It was her turn to look at him with surprise. "Lambeth."

"Oh."

"Have you heard of it?"

"I'm sure I have. I'm not sure how often I have actually been here, though. It doesn't seem overly familiar."

"Well, that would make sense," she said, taking a breath.

"But sometimes you need a different perspective to truly understand something."

She stopped in front of a building that was three storeys, with rows of matching square windows the only break in the red brick.

"Where are we?"

"The orphanage," she said, doing all she could to keep her expression neutral, as she turned to find him looking rather shocked. "I wanted to show you what happens when people are imprisoned for petty crimes."

"What does an orphanage have to do with such a thing? You can't tell me these children are criminals!"

"They are not — at least, most of them aren't," she said softly. "But many of their parents were. I spent two years of my life here, until I was old enough to fend for myself."

"Oh," he said without further comment, which made sense, for what else was there to say to that? He cleared his throat. "Is this fair, though, Georgie? I don't want to make these children feel as though I am simply here to stare at them with pity, or for you to teach me a lesson. I—"

"Don't be silly," she said with a hard look, annoyed that he would think she would ever do such a thing. "I come here every week. They're expecting me. *You* will be the surprise."

Before he could answer that, she was through the front door, and leaving him no choice but to follow her.

Cries of "Miss Jenkins!" greeted them.

Georgie grinned as the children ran up to her, and she took a moment to say hello to each of them. The girls and boys were of a wide range of ages, but she made sure she took as much time with the older ones as the young ones — they often needed just as much attention, if not more.

"How are the lessons going?" she asked the children, truly eager to know. She wished she could spend more time helping them, but thankfully they had good women and men here now who were doing all they could to help these children find themselves a better life than they had known so far.

They led her into their sitting area, where she greeted their caregivers, before settling down and pulling a book out of her bag.

"I've brought a new story for you," she said as they stared up at her eagerly. "It's about a princess and her prince who she's been waiting for. And I have a special surprise — I've brought a prince to come help read it to you!"

All of their faces turned toward Leo, who was standing, hesitatingly, at the doorway. He slowly approached, taking a seat beside Georgie with some obvious apprehension.

"I don't think I've been around many children," he murmured as he sat next to her, and she opened the book encouragingly.

"That's fine," she said. "All you have to do is read."

He began slowly, haltingly, but then soon warmed to his character, especially as the children seemed quite enamoured with his voice. Georgie couldn't blame them — it was engrossing to listen to, reminding her of warm, smooth chocolate flowing over her tongue. By the end, he was seemingly as shocked as anyone else listening when the princess ended up vanquishing the dragon and saving herself.

Afterward, the children clamoured toward him with questions. Rather than avoid them, he took the time to answer each one of them slowly, thoughtfully, with as much respect as he would any adult.

Georgie was just as enamoured as the rest of them, as she sat back and couldn't help but watch. After an hour she began to put away her things, and Leo came over to help her as the children returned to their lessons for the day.

"Do you see little Jack over there?" she asked.

He nodded.

"His father was transported for stealing a pair of gold

candlesticks from his employer. And Sally with the red braids?"

He didn't say or do anything this time, as though he didn't want to know.

"Her home was broken into. Her father was murdered and when her mother protected her, shooting one of the attackers, she was accused of murder. She is awaiting sentencing."

"But—"

"I know," Georgie said, her mouth in a grim line. "It's not fair. But there is no one to fight for these people."

"But you," Leo said quietly. "You do."

"I do what I can," she said, her hands forming fists in her frustration. "But it's not enough. It never will be. I can help one case at a time, one person at a time, but I don't have any power to make any lasting change. And now those who know nothing about these people are trying to make it even worse."

She turned to him, knowing her frustration and desperation were apparent, but unable to hide them any longer. "What am I supposed to do?"

He placed a hand on the small of her back, wishing he could do more, but not here, not surrounded by so many people. "I don't know, Georgie," he said softly, his eyes caressing her. "But whatever you need, I'm here."

She nodded curtly before they said farewell to the children, and then she led him back into the street.

"One more stop before we return."

"Very well," he said, unable to hide his apprehension. "Where are we going?"

"Bedlam."

* * *

WELL, Leo was sure about one thing — he had never before been to Bedlam.

As much as Georgie insisted she could look after herself, he stayed close by her side as they approached the Bethlehem Hospital for the insane. He knew all manner of people were treated here, but he still instinctively wanted to remain as close as he could. One never knew.

She knew the attendants, one of whom let her in with a smile, and Georgie explained that after she had gained their trust, they allowed her to see her mother about once a week. He followed her down a long passageway, through a gallery, women staring at them from cells as they walked.

"Here," she said, stopping, as the attendant allowed the two of them entry, and he followed Georgie silently before coming to a stop just inside the doorway of the small room which looked to be a visiting room of sorts.

Georgie rushed forward and embraced the woman within. She resembled Georgie, but not only was she older, she was considerably hardened. Dirty. But even through her stained face, her smile was warm, full, and genuine as she embraced Georgie, before pushing her back a step.

"Georgie. Still in one piece, I see."

"Of course, Mother," Georgie assured her.

"And you've brought a friend."

The woman's eyes swivelled to Leo, who took a step forward, unsure of what to say, but eventually finding politeness to greet her.

"Mrs. Jenkins. A pleasure to meet you."

That drew forward a laugh, one so similar to Georgie's, except hers ended with a cough and a bit of a wheeze. "That's the first time I've heard that in years. Now, what kind of friend are you to my Georgie?"

"Ah…" That was one question no amount of whatever

polite breeding Georgie was sure he had could possibly have prepared him for.

"Just a friend, Mother," Georgie said quietly. "I'm helping him find his way through a bit of a tight spot."

"I see," Mrs. Jenkins said. "Well, don't make any trouble for my Georgie, do you hear? And whatever you do, don't break her heart."

"Mother!"

"Well, it's true," Mrs. Jenkins said defensively, and Leo couldn't help but like the woman for her forthrightness. "You're a gem, Georgie."

She rolled her eyes at her mother before the two of them launched into conversation, Georgie catching her up on all of the goings-on in her life while Leo sat back and listened. When they finally began to take their leave, Mrs. Jenkins caught his arm and pulled him close.

"Watch out for her, will you?" she said, pleading in her eyes. "She always assures me she is fine but… she needs someone to look after her."

Leo looked intently into the woman's eyes, his response coming not from his lips but from somewhere deep within.

"I will, Mrs. Jenkins," he vowed. "You have my word."

CHAPTER 10

"*A*re you sure about this?"

Leo turned back and forth in front of the mirror in Georgie's bedroom, calling out to where she waited in the main room beyond. He wasn't entirely sure how he felt about stepping in here, and he hadn't been able to stop himself from staring at the bed with lustful thoughts running through his mind.

He had stood there for so long that Georgie had called out to ask him if all was well, and he had hurriedly dressed.

She knocked and at his assent she stepped through the door, coming up behind him in the mirror and staring at him, fixedly.

"Very dapper, my lord."

"I'm not sure if—"

"Oh, you are," she said curtly, and he realized it was not exactly something she admired. "I'm a good enough detective to determine that, at the very least."

He turned to her with narrowed eyes. "Don't tell me you are upset with yourself for not yet ascertaining my identity."

She turned from him, although she lifted her chin. "I

should be doing more. Marshall and I have been looking into the explosion along with the Thames Police, but everyone is ruling it an accident. The boat itself, however, had traveled far, all the way from, originally, New South Wales."

He frowned, having no recollection of travelling across the ocean. Surely he would remember… "It's not your fault. I haven't given you much opportunity, not allowing you to ask anyone about me," he said. "Hopefully tonight we'll determine something."

"Perhaps," was all she said, then she stepped toward the door. "Are you ready?"

He nodded, crossing the room to her in a couple of quick strides. "Before we go…" He couldn't stop himself. Could not keep from standing close behind her, allowing his breath to tickle the back of the neck, and he was pleased to see her shiver. "I cannot allow you to leave without telling you how beautiful you look tonight."

And beautiful she was. She was dressed the temptress, at least to him, in a red and black silk dress that hugged her in all the right places, showcasing beautifully sculpted shoulders and a creamy expanse of neck and collarbone. A matching red and black mask encircled her face, while she had left her hair to tumble down in rich, luxurious curls over both temples.

He was entranced and couldn't help but reach out just to see how one of those soft strands felt between his fingers.

It was like the very silk that encased her body.

And he matched, in his red waistcoat and black trousers and jacket.

"Thank you," she said, dipping her head. "You don't look so bad yourself."

"Just where did you find these clothes for tonight? Your role play friend again?"

Her cheeks turned as red as her dress.

"No, actually. Alice lent me these."

"Alice?"

She nodded. "A rather new friend, but a close one all the same. She's Mrs. Luxington, married to Benjamin Luxington, brother to the Marquess of Dorrington." She angled her head and asked, "Do those names mean anything to you?"

He frowned, searching his brain, but it seemed it was still as empty as it had ever been.

"No."

"No matter. If we do meet her, she is to be trusted. Although she may put you into one of those books of hers."

Before he could ask what Georgie meant, she was sailing out the door and he could only follow.

She was already calling a hack by the time he caught up, and he adjusted his mask in order to better see through the dimly lit night.

"We're not walking tonight?" he asked, teasing her, and she shook her head.

"Not tonight. The Keswicks may be unconventional merchants, but it still wouldn't seem right for us to *walk* up to the door. We shall stand out in a hired hack as it is, but I do not think either of us currently has the funds for a true carriage."

He nodded, leaning back against the seat, choosing to sit next to her, pressing his leg up against hers. It was a stolen touch, one that was innocent enough — as long as she didn't know what her very close presence was doing to his heart nor his sensibilities. He wiped at his brow, where a bead of sweat welled and threatened to fall.

He was nearing the point where, if he didn't recall his past, he was going to have to make a choice. Did he leave Georgie or try to move forward with her, possibly committing a sin against both her and a woman he couldn't remember?

Finally Georgie broke the silence with a clearing of her throat, moving her gaze away from the window to look at him.

"My thoughts were to enter the ballroom but to not make much of a scene. The mask covers most of your face, but if anyone there is intimately familiar with you, they will likely still recognize you. We will keep to the outskirts of the room, remaining in the shadows while you try to determine if anything is familiar. Unfortunately, the masks also mean that it might be more difficult for you to recognize anyone, but safety is of the utmost importance. Whatever you do, *do not dance.*"

"If only we knew just how dangerous it would be for me to be recognized."

"Well, I shouldn't like to risk your death again."

"Oh?" He couldn't help but wink at her, unsure whether she could see the gesture in the dim light. "Would you be upset if something were to happen to me?"

She straightened. "Well, of course. It would be my fault."

He let it rest there, although it warmed him within to think that she just might potentially care.

The journey wasn't far, and soon the hack came to a stop. Georgie actually allowed Leo to assist her out, and he smiled to himself at how naturally it felt for her gloved fingers to rest within his, even for a moment.

"Come." She surprised him when she kept a hold of his hand, tugging him away from the front doors and around the side. "We'll go in the garden doors so that we are not announced to our hosts."

He could do nothing but follow through the tree-lined yard around the back before she led him over to stairs and up to the terrace.

"You seem to be rather adept at sneaking through gardens."

"And just what are you insinuating, Mr. Nobleman?"

"I'm just teasing."

"I know," she said, looking back at him, and he was pleased to see she wore a grin. "It's my job. And I'm *usually* quite good at it."

"Have I diminished your abilities?"

"Something like that."

She led him through the doors, and as she had said, they found themselves on the outskirts. The ballroom was awhirl with couples, most dressed in vibrant colors that a masquerade apparently allowed them to don. As he unthinkingly reached out to a tray for a brandy, he realized quite quickly that Georgie was absolutely right — he was at home here. He felt comfortable, like this was a situation he had oft found himself in.

He looked over at Georgie and saw that she was watching him, a crook of her lips telling him that she knew what he was thinking and was pleased to find she was right.

It caused some turmoil in his belly at the realization they were at the point where they could accurately guess what one another was thinking without even trying. It was both unsettling and comforting in the same moment. It made no sense whatsoever, but then, neither did this entire situation with Georgie.

"Georgie!"

A dark-haired woman joined them, a man who was obviously her husband in tow. She immediately turned to Leo, looking at him with a great deal of interest. "Well, now, just who do we have here?"

"Alice," Georgie hissed, although she was laughing at her friend, who Leo smiled at politely. "This is Mr. Smith. A friend of a friend. There is no need to ogle him."

"My apologies, Mr. Smith. May I introduce my husband, Mr. Luxington?"

Luxington greeted Leo cheerily. He seemed a friendly enough sort, and his mask didn't hide much of his features, which were altogether unfamiliar.

"Are you new to London?" Luxington asked, to which Leo didn't provide a straight answer. "I am... reacquainting myself with the city," he said. "Miss Jenkins has been kind enough to provide her assistance."

"Well, the Keswick ball is the highlight for many through the year," Alice interjected, although she kept looking back and forth between him and Georgie with interest. "I wish Rose was here. She has returned to Lyme Regis already, though, and we likely won't see her until the wedding."

"Oh yes, the wedding!" Georgie exclaimed. "I had nearly forgotten."

"We shall have to make a plan. But first, Georgie, if Mr. Smith doesn't mind, Lord Ingersoll has been asking about you. I told him that as soon as I found you, I would ensure you would dance with him. In that dress, I am sure he will be most obliged."

"Oh, Alice, you know I can't—*don't* dance," Georgie was already shaking her head. "And Lord Ingersoll? What would he want to do with me?"

"He finds you intriguing."

"But—"

Before she could say anything further, a short but agreeable-enough looking young man stepped in front of them. "Miss Jenkins. Would you permit me this dance?"

"I—"

She looked around, lost for words, and Leo wasn't sure what his role was. He wanted nothing more than to forcefully rip her hand away from this gentleman's, but that would only draw unwanted attention to himself. Besides, who was he to ask anything of Georgie? He waved to the dance floor, granting his permission to go ahead.

"Not to worry about me," he said with a forced cheery smile. "I shall be fine here with your friends."

"Say, do I know you?" the young lord asked, peering at Leo, who took a step back in the shadows.

"You must have me confused with someone else."

Georgie raised her chin, nodding firmly before placing her hand in the lord's. "Let us try this, then," she said, allowing him to lead her out onto the dance floor, and Leo had to tamp down the growl that threatened to emerge.

Leo and the Luxingtons were soon joined by a couple Mrs. Luxington introduced as Madeline and Drake, a colleague of Georgie's, who Leo knew he should be greeting politely, but he currently had no time for either of them. He couldn't keep himself from watching Georgie as she spun around the floor in the arms of Ingersoll, whoever he was. She was talking to him, laughing with him, and before long he found he couldn't take it anymore as fists formed on either side of his legs.

"Excuse me," he said to the party and then continued on, back through the garden doors through which he'd arrived. He knew he was being rude as he pushed past people, but he didn't care. He had an overwhelming urge to get far from here, from his intrusion on Georgie's life, from this go-between that he couldn't find his way out of. He needed to leave. He needed to flee. He needed—

"Leopold Belmont," A voice seethed in his ear. "I didn't think it was possible. I thought you long dead."

Leo struggled in the man's grip, digging his fingers into the flesh of the forearm that encircled his throat, his gaze searching for onlookers, but he was too far into the dark garden.

"I am—" He gasped for air, his windpipe nearly choked off. "Consider me dead. Let me go. I'll leave you be, whoever you are."

The man laughed in his ear. "So you say. But I don't think so. Your very presence is too great a risk for me. A risk that I cannot allow."

"Who—who are you?"

"Oh, you don't recognize my voice? Has it been that long? A pity. Your brother makes a much more agreeable Lord Richmond, wouldn't you say?"

As the man spoke, Leo had stopped trying to fight him off, requiring more of his explanation, hoping that it would spark something within his memories, of who he was or what he could have possibly done to so anger the man. Leo was just preparing to launch the man over his head when suddenly the arm was gone, and he turned to determine just who had saved him and was shocked to find the man locked in a fistfight with none other than... Georgie. As the assailant came up behind her, she sent a hard elbow back into his nose, to which he immediately raised his hands as he stumbled backward. She turned in a swirl of finesse and made contact in his bollocks with her slippered foot. It might not have had as much of an effect as it would have had she had been wearing boots and breeches, but it was well-aimed and powerful and the man, dressed in formal trousers and jacket, was soon bent over.

"What do you think you are doing?" she seethed, leaning over, her hand coming to his hair as she lifted his masked face. Leo was still admiring the fact that she wasn't even breathing heavily. "Keep your hands off him."

"Need a lady to do your bidding, Ri—"

Before the man could finish the sentence, however, Leo stepped up to him and swung a punch right into the nose that was already bleeding. At the man's howl, guests began rushing to the balcony above them, and Leo grabbed Georgie's arm and hauled her back and away.

"You don't need to be involved in scandal," he murmured. "Let's go."

She chased after him, protest on her lips, but he wouldn't hear of it.

"It's not worth it helping me, Georgie," he said as they rounded the corner to the pavement out front, and it was his turn to haul her along as they looked for a hack on the road.

"Leo, slow down!" she called, grabbing onto his arm. "Why didn't you let him finish? He was going to say something. I think he knew who you were. No one cares if I am scandalous! I'm no one. We should go back. We should—"

He was already shaking his head. Maybe he didn't remember who he was or what he had done, but the more he learned about himself and his life, the less convinced he was that it was one he should be going back to. Who was he and what had he done to cause people to be so upset with him that they were out to kill him?

As much as Leo knew he needed answers, he had the sense that when they finally discovered who he was, Georgie would want nothing to do with him.

It seemed he was better off dead.

CHAPTER 11

*G*eorgie slept fitfully all night. Leo must be hiding something. While she didn't think he had captured any of his former memories, it was obvious that he knew *something* — something that he didn't want to share. Did he not trust her anymore? Or was the truth too much for him to bear?

It broke a small piece of her heart, for she was beginning to realize that she wanted to be the one who he turned to, the one with whom he shared his burdens, just as she had shared hers with him. She had showed him every piece of her life, damnit. The least he could do was allow her to help him — which wasn't at all possible if he wasn't willing to be open with her.

She dressed hurriedly, today in breeches and a shirt and jacket — she had best go check in at Bow Street— and exited her bedroom, prepared to tell him exactly what she thought.

Only to find that the room was empty.

Perhaps he had gone out to find breakfast, she mused, recalling with a smile that waded through her irritation at the memory of the meal he had made for her the other day. It had taken them an hour to clean up after him, but the effort had been worth it.

While she waited, she'd make coffee, something that he seemed to savour. It didn't escape her notice that she rather enjoyed preparing something for him, which was not at all like her. She was far too used to looking after only herself.

But when she crossed to the counter, she found it — the note, right beside the kettle, where she couldn't have missed it.

Georgie,

His scrawl was dark, heavy, and it made her heart ache to read his words upon the page.

I can hardly believe that I am leaving you, but I find I am left with no choice. I never should have put you in danger to begin with. I know you are likely shouting at me that you can look after yourself, and you are right. I know that far too well. But the longer I stay, the more at risk you will be — from my enemies and from me.

I am sorry to tell you this through a note, but it seems that I am not a man who enjoys saying goodbye. I hope someday in the future we are able to meet again under better circumstances.

Until then, I thank you for everything.

Leo

Georgie replaced the letter upon the scarred wooden table with shaking hands. It felt as though she had been punched in the stomach, and she gripped the edges of the tabletop in an effort to steady herself. He had left her. In the middle of the night. Like a coward.

She banged her fist down upon the table, causing all of the utensils upon it to jump with a crash.

"Bloody bastard!" she shouted into the air, allowing the anger to overcome her, if only to keep the angst at bay. She hardly knew Leo whatever-his-name was, and yet his sudden removal left a hole in her heart and in her life that she hadn't even known was within.

For this was her own fault. She had failed him. She had been so caught up with sharing her life and trying to get close to him that she had practically ignored partaking in the investigation she had promised him, the investigation that kept the two of them together.

But none of it mattered, for now he was gone.

She picked up the cup he had always used for his coffee and swung her hand back to throw it across the room, but stopped herself just in time. The momentary satisfaction wouldn't be enough to make up for the time she would have to spend cleaning it up.

Damn practicality.

She was about to turn away when she saw something gleaming beside her own cup, and she stopped, inching her fingers closer to grab it.

Leo's medallion. She palmed it in her fist, causing the metal to dig into the soft skin of her hand, but she welcomed the sharp pain with a hiss. Why had he left this here? Had he really thought she would want such a reminder of him?

Well, she thought as she threw it back down to the countertop, nothing left to do but actually return to work and do something useful. She had not only been away under the guise of her focus on this one case for days, but she would be leaving shortly for her friend Rose's wedding in Lyme Regis.

At least Rose and Perry had found happiness. Or as much as they could, with Perry's impending earldom in the future, a life neither of them wanted.

Georgie sighed. Circumstances of birth were such a bitch.

She shrugged into her jacket, leaving without a backward glance toward the place by the fire where Leo had made his bed. She didn't think her little home would ever be the same again.

* * *

LEO SLOUCHED against the brick wall, staring out at the bustling street in front of him. He received a few glances, but most people walked on by him without a care, busy wrapped up in their own thoughts and challenges for the day.

He ran a hand over his face as melancholy settled over his shoulders like a cloak of dread.

He'd had no other choice but to leave. For he was falling in love with Georgie.

A woman who was far too good for him, who would never have him, not when she knew who he was and what he was capable of. He was not only a man she would despise, but a man who wasn't free to love her.

If only he could completely start over. But that was impossible. Not here. Not in London. His recognition last night meant that it would only be a matter of time until his death was sought again.

If he stayed, he would be putting Georgie in even more danger than he already had. He hoped that she would understand why he had left, that she wouldn't hold too much anger in her heart.

If they were meant to be, then someday they would find their way back together. It was all that he had to hold onto.

Finally, the door he had been watching cracked open, and Georgie stepped out. Back in her breeches today, he noticed with a sad smile. She began walking in the opposite direction from where he stood, and he followed her with his eyes as long as he could. She walked quickly, as though she was trying to put as much distance as she could between herself and her home. Her face, in that brief moment she had turned his way, had seemed troubled, angry.

Because of him.

He prayed, if nothing else, she would be mad enough to

let this go and try to put him behind her. He didn't want her to put herself in any further danger because of him. It was why he had done the only thing he knew how, and had left her behind.

He turned on his heel now.

He had a purpose. He had to surreptitiously access the funds he needed to find a place for himself to live, at least until he figured this out. He couldn't put anyone in additional danger. Everyone thought him dead, and it was far better that he remain in such a state for now. He just had to hope that news of his return from the other night wouldn't spread too fast.

For this morning, when he awoke, everything had changed.

He had awoken Leopold Archibald Belmont, Viscount Richmond, the future Earl of Sheriden.

He had remembered.

And now that he had? He wished the truth had never returned.

* * *

THREE WEEKS later

"WHAT'S WRONG WITH YOU?" Alice demanded.

"What are you talking about?" Georgie forced a smile.

It had been three weeks since she had last seen Leo. Three weeks in which she had tried to put him out of her mind. Three weeks in which she couldn't stop missing him.

She pushed the thoughts of him aside, at least for the moment. This was their last night in Lyme Regis. She and her friends had traveled the considerable journey here a week ago. After enjoying Rose and Perry's wedding, they had stayed on a day longer than most of the guests, for they assumed it would be some time until they were able to see Rose again. It was Georgie's second visit here, and she appreciated the time away from London. She had spent nearly her entire life there, barely leaving the city's borders. She could understand why Rose and Perry so loved this place. It was tranquil, beautiful, the ocean lapping against the shore providing a brief respite from all of the busyness of her life and mind.

A mind that was filled with a man she had no business thinking about.

"Alice, leave her alone," Madeline murmured. "Georgie is allowed to feel something besides her usual cheer."

"But she has been like this for weeks now. Ever since the Keswick ball, when the mysterious Mr. Smith accompanied her."

"This has nothing to do with Mr. Smith," Georgie interjected, even as she could feel Rose fidgeting on the other side of her. "Now hush, Rose and Perry are waiting to speak."

"Thank you all for coming," Rose said, looking around the dinner table.

"Of course," Alice said with a wide smile. "We wouldn't have missed it for anything."

"And thank you, Georgie," Rose said, surprising her when she reached out to take her hand. "I know that it is difficult to get away."

"There are crimes to be solved all over England," Georgie said with a smile. "Why not in Lyme Regis?'

"Let's hope things are a little quieter here — for that is what I love about it," Rose said. "How have things been at Bow Street?"

"Quiet, surprisingly," Georgie said with a shrug. "I've actually become rather bored over the past while."

Since Leo left.

"Don't say that," Drake said, wagging his finger as he shook his head vehemently. "You know what happens when we say something like that, Georgie. It's not a good idea."

Georgie couldn't help but laugh at that and realized that this had been good for her, being here with her friends. As long as she didn't have too many moments alone when the thoughts she had been resisting tried to creep in, she would be fine.

"You are far too superstitious, Drake. I'm simply telling the truth of how things are. Let go of your worries and let's enjoy this night away from work."

Drake nodded, although his concern was obvious, but forgotten as the seven of them were served dinner and enjoyed a riotous first round of toasts.

Then suddenly the door burst open, slamming against the wall to reveal a very damp, very bedraggled woman.

"Is that Lady Anne?" Georgie murmured to Alice, who nodded, her eyes wide as they all stared at the woman.

Lady Anne had been present at the wedding, but they had all thought she was to leave today. It must have been strange for her to have been at the wedding that easily could have been her own.

"Lady Anne?" Rose said, standing and crossing to her as the rest of them stared on. "What are you doing here? Are you all right?"

"I had to return to find you," she said with a cry, her eyes, wild now, dancing between them all. "There's something you have to know, Perry."

"Yes?"

"Leo is alive!"

Georgie's fork clattered to her plate.

While distinctly aware of the increasing murmurs around her, for Georgie, everything had gone quiet, the moment frozen in time around her.

She stared at the woman in front of her. The blond woman, as delicately beautiful as they come despite her current state, had apparently had such a love match with Perry's brother. Georgie realized now she had never known his first name. He had been Lord Richmond.

Lord Richmond. Leo. Leopold Belmont. Her stomach whirled with sudden nausea, her mind racing back to the man in the gardens. He had nearly called him as such. And Leo... Leo had stopped him. But why? Had he known and had he been preventing her from discovering just who he was?

"What's wrong?" Alice hissed, poking her in the side, and Georgie could only shake her head mutely.

Her first thought should have been elation at discovering just who Leo was. If she could locate him once more, he could return home and take his rightful place.

A place away from her. With Lady Anne by his side.

Good God.

She tuned out all the chatter around her, until she heard Perry questioning Anne as to just how she knew this to be true, and Georgie then focused her attention once more.

"My cousin said he saw him at the Keswick Ball. I told him that he must surely be mistaken, for it was a masquerade this year, and perhaps there was just another man in attendance who looked like Leo. He didn't seem convinced, but then one of his friends confirmed that he saw him — without a mask — in the gardens."

As much as Georgie wanted to escape this room and all of the secrets it was slowly revealing to her, the detective in her persisted.

"Who is this friend — your cousin's friend?" she asked, as they all looked at her in curiosity as to why she would care about such a detail.

"Lord Lovelace."

"Lord Lovelace?" Drake practically growled, even as Benjamin stood and began pacing the room.

"My brother has mentioned him a time or two," Benjamin said, running a hand through his hair, "and it has never been with any particular happy sentiment. I'm not sure what he did, but it must have something to do with Freddie. Miles won't speak of it."

"Would Lord Lovelace have any reason to lie?" Madeline asked, but none of them seemed to have an answer.

Anne was wringing her hands in the doorway, and Rose walked over to her, taking her by the hand and sitting her down on her own chair, right next to Georgie.

"Anne," Rose said firmly, kneeling down in front of her. "Are you all right?"

Anne nodded quickly. "I think so. Shocked, is all."

"Why are you out in the rain by yourself?"

"It's pouring outside, and I ran from the carriage. My mother accompanied me, but she refused to emerge into the rain. We received the missive from my cousin as we were about to depart for London. I insisted we stop here first, for Perry had to know."

She looked up at Rose's husband, who was still leaning against the wall, shock on his face.

"I can hardly believe it," Perry murmured. "After all this time. But where was he and why hasn't he come home?"

"I think I can help with that," Georgie said, and they all turned to look at her.

Well, yes, she could actually tell them some of what they needed to know, although she couldn't answer where he had been for an entire year prior to his return. But how could she share any of Leo's secrets when she didn't even know what had taken him from his family in the first place? She had to find him first, and get to the bottom of all of this.

"I'll do everything I can to find him," she promised both Perry and Alice.

"As will I," Drake said, and Georgie closed her eyes for a moment. She really wished Drake would stay out of this, but how could she explain to her fellow Bow Street detective why she needed to do this on her own?

She would have to figure that out later. For now, she just nodded with a tight smile.

"Well," Rose said, patting Anne's knee. "You must be ever so happy."

Anne looked up, then around the room, her eyes shining with unshed tears, her lip quivering. "I am pleased that he is alive, if what my cousin says is true. Leo was quite a force and a good man, deep in his heart. But there's just one thing," she practically whispered. "I don't love him anymore."

CHAPTER 12

*L*eo would never have thought that this was the life he would be leading.

He had broken into one of the finest homes in Mayfair. Yes, it was his own, but no one would believe him if he were to be caught. He hardly looked the part of future earl anymore, in his second-hand shirt, trousers, and jacket that had gone too many days without laundering.

And he had stolen money and clothing. Again, it was his own. But, still, anyone finding him in possession of such things while in his current state would surely wonder how a man such as he had come to find it all. And now here he was, renting a room at a disreputable inn, hoping he wouldn't have to spend much time here, but unsure just when he would be able to return to his home and his life.

He ran a hand through his hair, forcing himself to conjure up an image of Lady Anne Fitzgerald, the woman he had apparently loved and was going to marry.

But every time he thought of his future wife, all he could think about was Georgie.

He walked over to the washbasin, splashing water on his face before donning black clothes for his evening's activities. Lord Lovelace had attacked him in the garden — and it was not his first attack, Leo thought grimly. It still smarted that the man had bested him over a year ago now, but then he had gone and stolen a year of Leo's life along with it. Now Leo had to find out if Lovelace had any accomplices, and determine how to prove Lovelace's guilt before Leo could completely return to his old life. For he had to make sure that they would never threaten him or his family again.

And then... he supposed he would become Lord Richmond.

He wasn't sure if he could actually follow through and marry Anne anymore. He could do so out of duty, he supposed, but out of love? Well, he didn't know if that was there any longer. He still held some affection for her, but now he knew that what he had felt for her before wasn't love. Love was what had been growing for Georgie.

Except one thing he knew for certain? Georgie wouldn't marry him. Not when she found out who he was and what he had done.

And find out she would. These secrets always had a way of revealing themselves.

He slipped from the inn, his hat low over his face. He had found lodging in Cheapside, not far from Georgie's place. He told himself that it was pure coincidence, but he couldn't even lie to himself about that. He wanted to be close to her. Even if he couldn't actually touch her, he might just see her from a distance. It was a risk, for there was a chance he could run into her, but he was as careful as could be.

He waved down a hack to take him to Mayfair, unable to push away the memory of his ride with Georgie in such a vehicle. If only he had known then that it was one of the last times they would be together, he would have savoured the moment far more than he had. He would have been grateful just to be with her, rather than desperately wishing for more.

The hack came to a stop a block away from the Lovelace townhouse, and he paid the man before sending him off. He crept down the street and turned into the yard, his pulse beating rapidly at the thought of what he was about to do.

"Need some help?"

He just managed to stifle the yelp that threatened to emerge, and swiveled around to find a figure in the shadows. He couldn't make out the features or the person hiding in the dark, but he would know that voice anywhere.

"Georgie," he hissed. "What do you think you are doing here?"

"What am *I* doing here?" she stepped out into the dim light. "I hardly think that I am the one that should be answering questions. You have a lot of explaining to do."

She took a shaky breath, and he was pleased to see that she was just as affected by their reunion as he was.

"I know this isn't the time or the place to discuss this, but judging by the fact you are here at Lord Lovelace's, I am assuming you already know that you are Lord Leopold Belmont."

He could only nod. "I do."

"When did you remember?"

"You're right. This is not the time or place for this."

"When did you remember?"

He sighed, running his hand through his hair. "The morning after the masquerade."

"I see." She nodded succinctly, obviously upset. "You wouldn't want to stick around and tell me. Prefer to just leave a note. Easier that way, I suppose."

"Georgie—"

"It doesn't matter," she said, holding up a hand, refusing

94

to hear anymore. "I would leave you alone to do whatever it is you think you're going to do, but I made a promise that I would find you. So find you I did."

"How—"

"I'll tell you later. Now, what are we doing at Lord Lovelace's?"

"I have my own reasons for being here, Georgie," he said, advancing closer toward her now. "I have no idea how you knew I would be here, but you need to let this be. I have to take care of this on my own."

"You can say that all you want, but the truth is, you have no right to enter this house without permission. What will you do about it?"

He stepped closer. She didn't move back, but lifted her chin to meet his gaze. She was just the right height. Tall for a woman, which was perfect for him, as high he stood himself.

"Don't test me."

"Georgie," he said, summoning all of his charm as he tucked an index finger underneath her chin. "You would never turn me in."

She levelled him with her gaze. "I don't even know you."

He dropped his finger abruptly, as though her skin had burned him. She was right. She didn't know him. Not who he truly was.

"Very well," he grunted. "You can come with me. But we must be very careful."

"Obviously." He could practically hear her rolling her eyes. "How many times have you broken into a house before?"

"Once."

"Your own?"

"Yes," he looked over at her in surprise. "How did you know?"

"Your parents contacted me and Drake, telling us that

there had a been a break-in while they were away at Perry's wedding."

His head snapped toward her at that and he grabbed her arm. He hadn't heard what he thought he had heard — had he?

"What did you just say?"

"I said, your parents contacted me, and—"

"Georgie," he said, restraining himself from shaking her, for he knew she was aware of exactly what he meant. "Did you say Perry was married?"

"He was," she said with a quick nod.

"To whom?"

His heart beat quickly. Had Perry married Anne? The selfish side of him was almost hoping that he had, for if he had married Anne, that would mean Leo was free. Except that would also mean that Perry had tied himself to a woman for no true justification, and that Leo had unintentionally stolen his brother's true chance for happiness. Oh, God. He ran a hand over his face, peering between his fingers to find Georgie watching him with a great deal of interest.

"Not to worry," she finally said curtly, "he didn't marry your Anne. He married Rose Ellis, a woman he met in Lyme Regis."

"Oh," Leo said, his shoulders sinking back down, away from his ears. "Thank goodness."

"Yes. Now, are we going to stand here in the shadows waiting to be discovered all night, or are we going in?"

"I've been here before," Leo said, taking her hand as he pulled her around to where he knew there were garden doors. She tried to jerk her hand away, but he kept it tight in his grasp. "I don't know whether they will have locked the back doors."

"It would be foolish not to."

He shrugged. "People become complacent, at least in these neighborhoods."

"What exactly are you going to do when you go inside?"

"I need to get to Lord Lovelace's study, see if I can find proof that he orchestrated my disappearance. I would also like to know just who he is working with."

"Then what are you going to do?"

"Convince him how bad it would be for his health to continue."

He heard the edge in his voice, saw Georgie's hard stare, and he quickly averted his gaze. This was why it was best she not know any more about who he truly was and the lengths he would go to in order to get his way.

Especially when that way was nothing at all she would approve of — but, in fact, the opposite.

"Let's go."

He led her up the steps, finally releasing her gloved hand, lifting his to try the door handle.

Locked.

"Damn it," he cursed, and she nudged him out of the way with her hip. She was similarly dressed to him, in black breeches, boots, and jacket, her hair tied back away from her face in a braid that roped around her shoulders to stretch down her neck and into the cleavage of her shirt.

"Move," she instructed, and he swallowed hard, nearly completely undone by both her delectable curves and the way she took command.

He had always thought he would want a woman who was meek, eager to please him and do his will.

How wrong he had been.

She took a few tools out of her jacket pocket before kneeling in front of the handle and going to work.

"Do you have any reason to believe that anyone will be

home or awake?" she asked softly, and he crouched down next to her to watch how she was turning the lock with the small metal instrument.

"I have reason to believe that Lord and Lady Lovelace are out at the theatre tonight."

"How do you know?"

"Lovelace always enjoys this particular opera singer."

"I see."

Leo enjoyed the fact that she wasn't an innocent miss, but that he could speak freely with her without worry that she would faint away at the merest mention of anything distinctly scandalous.

"The staff will be our only concern, then."

"Yes, but hopefully they have no reason to be in Lovelace's study. It will simply be a matter of finding our way there."

"What room is this?" she asked as the handle turned with a click, and he could have kissed her.

"This is the parlor, I believe."

"How many times have you been here?" She ignored the hand he provided, rising on her own.

"Once."

"When?"

"A few years ago."

The look she gave him made him feel a complete fool again, but there was nothing to be done about it as he pushed open the door and waved a hand in.

"After you."

It was a mistake. For then he had to watch her beautiful bottom in those tight breeches as she walked by him.

The parlor was dark, the hearth unlit. Georgie stood on one side, waving him behind her, her index finger over her lips. Leo nodded as she peeked her head around the inside door. The corridor must have been empty, for she gestured within, and he took the lead now, stepping through the door and showing her where he thought the study was. This time the door was, thankfully, open, and she slipped in behind him as he lit a lamp so that they could see what they were doing.

"Now what? We simply search through his things?"

Leo shrugged. "That was my plan."

She didn't seem particularly impressed. "Fine, but hurry," she said. "Then we'll take what we need and read it away from here."

"What if he finds it gone?"

"Do you care?"

"I suppose not."

"What exactly are we looking for?"

Leo rubbed his forehead, unsure of how much he could explain to her at the moment.

"Evidence. Anything that refers to me, obviously, perhaps to meeting with me at the Red Lion Club, or a transport ship bound for New South Wales."

She stopped, her lips parted in surprise. "What happened?"

"I'll tell you later."

"I have so many questions."

"I know."

They worked in silence for a time, the two of them methodically together, Leo looking through one side of the desk, Georgie the other.

Georgie nearly slammed a door in frustration, and Leo glanced over to find her glaring at him.

"It is becoming increasingly frustrating searching with one eye closed."

"What do you—"

"How am I supposed to know what I am looking for if you will not tell me the full story and what is between you and Lovelace?"

He looked back down at the drawer in front of him, refocusing on his search. "I didn't ask you to come here."

"And I didn't ask you to float in on a board down the Thames, but you did."

A notice captured his attention, and he picked it up, quickly skimming his eyes down the page. Here it was. Some information he could use.

"What is it?" Georgie asked, circling around behind his shoulder.

"It's a notice demanding that Lovelace repay his debts."

"From who?"

"A man he should have no business dealing with."

"You are being quite aggravating."

"Sorry," Leo said hastily, shoving the page into his shirt. "But I can use this against him, perhaps to bribe or blackmail him."

"Do you really think that is the answer here?"

"It might be the only answer."

He continued rifling through the desk drawers, and Georgie, apparently frustrated at her inability to find anything or know what she was looking for, followed after him, tidying up the papers as he went.

"What about this?" she asked.

"What?"

"He keeps a calendar here. A diary." She set it upon the desk, rifling back through it.

"When did you meet with him?"

"What timing are we looking for?"

"About a year ago."

"This is it."

"Perfect."

She began running her finger over the pages, but just then there was a footstep outside the door.

They looked at one another in horror, and then Georgie blew out the candle, picked up the book, and dove under the desk with Leo just as the door clicked open.

CHAPTER 13

"*I* don't have much time."

It must have been Lovelace's voice that floated down to where they huddled beneath the desk. They had naturally settled into a position of Georgie sitting tucked between Leo's bent legs. It was far from ideal, and yet it seemed to be the only way they would properly fit. Georgie took a breath, trying to calm her rapidly beating heart. She liked to tell herself that it was from the precariousness of their situation and not her proximity to Leo.

His breath brushed against her neck and the back of her ear, causing her to shiver as the voices neared.

"I told Margaret I was unwell when I left, and she will return with her brother and his wife."

"Not like you, to miss seeing Victoria Weatherington — on stage or off."

"I'll see much more of her later. Now, to the matter at hand. We know that Richmond is alive."

"Yes."

The evil in the other man's tone had Georgie clutching

Leo's thigh despite her misgivings at allowing herself such familiarity.

"How is this possible? I saw you kill him over a year ago."

"Apparently he wasn't fully dead."

"Have you seen him since the Keswick's ball? Can we be absolutely sure it was him?"

"Without a doubt."

"Where has he been since then?"

"I am hoping he will stay dead and buried, that the threat of his demise will be enough."

A snort resounded. "Lovelace. How stupid are you?"

Georgie felt Leo nodding in agreement.

"The past no longer matters," the second man continued. "I have heard there was another sighting of him. We need to decide what we are going to do, and we need to decide quickly, before this gets out of hand."

"What do you suggest?"

"We hire someone to find him and be rid of him."

"We tried that before, to hide the body. That obviously did not work."

"I know. The man said that when he went to throw him in the Thames, he realized the bugger apparently still had breath in him. Didn't want to kill a peer so he hid him on a transport ship, hoping he'd be dead before he was discovered. I wouldn't be overly concerned about the duel, but this…"

Georgie's eyes widened at the thought of Leo left to die. That he had managed to survive it was a miracle. That he was still here… her fingers tightened on his leg, until he flinched, forcing her to realize that she must have been hurting him, and she let go.

"Fine," the other man said. "Have the same man do the work again. He may have been unsuccessful, but the less people that know about this, the better."

"Marbury… I do question if it's worth it."

Tense silence reigned. "Do you want to go before the House for attempted murder? Dueling is illegal and you were the one to strike. This is one of the only crimes that can hang a peer. That and treason."

"No. Of course I do not want that."

"Well, then. We have to silence Richmond before this comes to light. Understood?"

"Very well," Lovelace grumbled. "I'll contact my man. Is that all?"

"It's everything."

"I'll keep you updated."

"See that you do."

Footsteps retreated, and Georgie took a deep breath, waiting another moment after the door clicked before she slowly scooted from beneath the massive mahogany desk, the blood rushing back into her legs when she stood. She cringed at the tingling sensation, before it finally receded.

She heard a couple of Leo's bones pop as he slowly pushed himself to standing.

"We've got what we need now," he whispered in her ear as he took hold of her elbow. "Let's go."

She looked down at the old diary before her, tucking it into her own jacket before following Leo to the door.

"We can't go down the corridor again," she said. "It's too risky, not now that we know Lovelace is home and the staff are likely preparing everything for him."

"So what do you suggest?"

She crossed the room, looking out the window, then nodded.

"This way."

She hefted the window up, swinging her leg over the ledge to crawl out, when Leo placed a hand on her shoulder. Damn it, why did his touch still fill her with a tingling sensation that rushed through her veins to the very place she ached for him?

"If we are going to jump out a window, allow me to do so first."

"Very well."

She stepped back and swept her hand out, and he gave her a look as if to say "watch this," his masculine, smug grin firmly in place. She raised an eyebrow and simply watched as he swung fluidly out the window — and right into a rose bush.

"Ouch!" he yelped, and she stuck her head out the window, shushing him. His pride was going to get them caught. She swung out the window herself, careful to avoid the bush that had captured Leo in its snares, and then the two of them inched their way along the wall out toward the street beyond.

"How did you get here?" Georgie asked, and Leo answered, "A hack."

She nodded. "Then we must find another."

They continued until they found the main road, and before Leo could say anything, she gave the driver the address of the inn where Leo was staying. He stared at her in shock, and now it was her turn to grin smugly.

"I am a better detective than I portrayed when we last spent time together," she said as they climbed in. "But the fact that I was able to find you so easily means that you are not safe in the inn. We will go collect your things and then return to my rooms."

"No," he said, shaking his head before she even finished speaking. "I cannot stay with you again."

"I know it is not ideal," she admitted. "You are betrothed to another and if anyone ever found out about our living situation, there would be serious repercussions. However, I can't think of a better way to keep you safe."

He snorted. "I am a grown man. I don't need you to look after me."

She fixed her gaze on him. "That may be so, but you still need somewhere to hide where no one is apt to find you. My rooms are your best option at the moment, whether you like it or not."

He quite obviously had no wish to spend any further time with her now that he was aware that he was not just a member of the nobility, but a future earl, one who had a bride and much greater responsibilities awaiting him.

She shouldn't care. She should let him stay at his inn and risk getting himself killed, leave him to figure this out for himself.

But she didn't have it within her to allow someone she cared about be put in harm's way.

For, damnit, she did care about him, as much as she tried not to.

"I am not the man you think I am," he said, as though reading her thoughts. "You don't know me."

"I do not know Lord Richmond, no," she said swiftly. "But I do know who you are, Leo. You may not have had your memories, but that doesn't mean that you aren't still the same man who I brought into my home upon a plea of mercy. I trusted you then, and I still trust you now."

"You shouldn't."

She shrugged. "Be that as it may, I do."

The hack trundled to a stop, and Leo fixed her with a stare as he seemed to fight a battle within him. Finally he sighed, apparently realizing that she was even more stubborn than he.

"Fine," he said tersely. "I will go get my things."

* * *

THEY EACH HAD SO much to say to one another that it seemed nearly impossible to know just where to begin.

They had returned to Georgie's rooms, and it was odd, Leo mused, that stepping through this door felt more like coming home than returning to his own family's house actually had.

He quickly realized why that was.

Because of the woman herself, as loath as he was to admit it, for there was absolutely nothing he could do about it.

They had taken up seats in front of the fireplace. They likely should both be retiring to bed, but neither of them seemed particularly inclined.

The normally talkative Georgie seemed bent on silence, and Leo didn't like it. Not one bit.

"Tell me of my brother," he finally began. "How do you know him?"

"He seems fine. Happy. I do not know him well," she said, stirring the coffee in her hand, holding it close as though it could warm her all the way through — something he longed to be doing himself. "I actually know his wife, Rose. We met through Alice."

"I see."

"The world can be dreadfully small sometimes, can't it?" she asked pensively, looking into the fire, not meeting his gaze. He had never seen this side of her before, and he wasn't sure he particularly liked it. He preferred the side that threw caution to the wind, that took home a strange man in order to save him, that jumped out of study windows and raced down the streets in breeches. "Especially London."

"Yes, it can."

"Lady Anne knows you're alive," she said, finally turning that brown stare upon him. "We were in Lyme Regis, at Greywater. It's where Perry and Rose have taken residence."

"Perry always did like it there," he said, ignoring her first words.

"Yes," she said with a tight smile. "We were dining together on our final night before departing for London when Lady Anne arrived with the information of your resurrection, supplied by her cousin, who is, apparently, friends with Lord Lovelace."

"Her cousin," Leo said, holding his body firm so that he didn't show her just how angry he was, "was the man in Lovelace's study tonight."

"Oh?" Georgie raised her eyebrows and sipped her coffee. "Well, that makes things particularly interesting."

"Doesn't it, though?"

"Anyway, she told us all that Leo — you — were alive. I hadn't actually known your name — that is, the name of the former Lord Richmond, Perry's brother — until that time. Suddenly it all came together. What I didn't know was whether you had any idea of your true identity. Now I know."

"Now you know. After Lovelace said my name that night, it all began coming back. How did you find me?"

"It wasn't particularly hard. Once I realized you had stolen your own money, I thought of where you could possibly afford that would still be of a close location to where you would need to access, and then I asked my contacts and the innkeepers. You were soon recognized. I followed you to Lovelace's."

"Why didn't you just approach me?"

"I wanted to see what you were up to."

"I see. Did you tell anyone I was alive?"

She studied him for a moment before eventually shaking her head. "No. I didn't know yet what danger might be threatening you and didn't think it was my place to tell your family until I spoke to you."

"And now?"

"Now, I just don't know what to do with you." She let out a long, slow exhale. "I think we should bring in Drake to help."

"No."

"He will be discreet," she said firmly. "He has a greater range of access to contacts than I do. But beside that, I know he can help, and he's looking for you, anyway."

Leo folded his arms across his chest and studied the determined set of her chin. He had the feeling that Georgina Jenkins was not used to people saying no to her.

"Unless…" she continued.

"Yes?"

"You want to tell me just what it is that you are hiding from me."

"I'm not hiding anything from you."

Just that he was secretly everything she hated. If he told her the full truth of the matter, it would lead to the conclusion of the story — that he was the very man she despised.

"How did you survive such severe injuries?"

He closed his eyes as he remembered the pain, sure he would die and all due to an ill-advised duel with Lovelace. He would, however, do it again in a heartbeat.

"There was a physician on board to see to the illnesses and injuries that arose. It's a long journey. Very long. When I finally convinced everyone I was not on the manifest, they provided me some extra care." Grinning, he offered a shrug. "Then there was my stubborn will to survive."

"And then?"

"I learned from them. When we arrived in New South Wales, I convinced them that if they allowed me to return with them, I would work my way back, make myself useful, and that, if I was who I said I was, I would make it worth their while."

"And then the explosion."

He nodded slowly. "Can you believe after all that time, the damn ship would explode so close to London? It's hard to believe everyone made it off."

"Including you."

He nodded. "Including me."

They sat in silence as she studied him, the tension gathering in the air between them.

"Fine, then," she finally said, breaking the silence. "I will ask Drake to come meet with us tomorrow."

He sighed and rubbed his forehead, accepting that he wasn't going to win without conceding something, though he most certainly couldn't tell her the full truth.

"How was Lady Anne?"

Georgie straightened, her knuckles turning white as she wrapped them tightly around the cup.

"She is well, actually."

"That's good to hear."

Their conversation was stilted. Awkward. Which made sense, for the air was filled with a desirous tension that they both couldn't be rid of, not with Lady Anne between them.

"What was her reaction to my apparent return to life?"

Georgie wouldn't meet his gaze again, looking back into the fire.

"I think you should speak to her yourself."

"Georgie, the whole point of this is for me to stay away and keep everyone safe. Hell, I shouldn't even be here, but—"

She twisted her head and cast her gaze upon him once more. "She deserves to know the truth, and she likely has much to say to you. First, she thought you were dead and now her entire life is on hold until she finds you. That's not fair to her."

His shoulders dropped down as he was properly chastised.

"You're right. Of course you're right. Is there a way we can set something up with the utmost discretion?"

"Actually…" she stretched her long legs out before her, "I was thinking that perhaps the best place to go is exactly where no one would expect."

"Which is?"

"Go home. Walk right in the front door."

CHAPTER 14

They decided, however, that the front door likely wasn't the best idea.

But the setting still was.

Georgie stared up at the house before her.

So this was where Leo lived. Where he had spent all of his time in London.

Her own rooms could likely fit into the drawing room alone. And this was only one of their homes. What did one do with so much space?

Well, it wasn't as though she was about to find out.

She was beginning to understand part of the reason why Rose had at first been so apprehensive about marrying Perry.

"I've spoken with the butler," Georgie said. "He agreed to let us in through the servants' entrance."

"He did?" Leo's deep voice murmured in her ear, and she both loved and hated the tremor it sent down her spine.

Leo sounded surprised, and Georgie understood why. The butler had been most trepidatious when she had approached him as an officer from Bow Street, but Georgie could be persuasive when she wanted to be. She might not be the most lovely or coquettish, but she was able to determine what would have meaning to someone and then use it to get her way.

"Well, if you can convince Collins of such suspicious schemes, then I wouldn't put anything past you."

"No," Georgie agreed, "it does not serve people well to underestimate me."

He gave her a look that told her he was somewhat chagrined for having done so himself. Good. As long as he had learned his lesson.

They were dressed in ill-fitting but appropriate clothing for door-to-door food merchants, carrying the day's food stores between them. Georgie was in men's clothing, even her hair today tucked underneath her hat.

She could only hope that Leo's baggy clothing and old, ragged cap dropped low over his forehead were enough to convince anyone who might be watching the house that he was no one to fear.

As they approached the servants' entrance, Leo suddenly froze, and Georgie recognized his uncertainty. Not only was he seeing his family again after far too long, but he was entering through the servants' entrance, something he had likely never done before.

Georgie decided it was time for her to take the lead, at least for now.

"Keep your hat low," she murmured. "Collins knows to try to keep this quiet from the rest of the staff. The less people who know, the better."

"And my family?"

"Collins tells me they were quite relieved, although somewhat suspicious, at the thought of finally seeing you after waiting so long for your return."

He nodded curtly, and she saw the guilt washing over his face.

"You have nothing to worry yourself over. None of this was your fault. And once you returned, you were only doing what you thought was best for their safety," she said, and he turned morose eyes upon her.

"An entire year of my life. Gone. And am I even doing the right thing now upon my arrival?"

She didn't have the answer to that, but what she did know was that Leo, his family, and Anne wouldn't get anywhere by sitting around and waiting for something to happen to them.

Besides, it was time that Leo spoke with Anne. It wasn't Georgie's place to betray Anne's confidence, and they needed to sort this out between them. If Anne loved Clark as she said she did, then she needed to be allowed to move on. And as for Leo, well, that was another matter entirely.

Georgie typically wasn't one to be overly impressed by wealth, but she couldn't help her gaze from wandering over all of the splendour as they made their way through the house to a smaller room in the back. She had suggested a more private parlor or study, where they wouldn't be disturbed and where fewer of the staff would have reason to enter.

"In here, Miss Jenkins. Lord Richmond."

Lord Richmond. Her heart ached. She wanted her Leo back, but she was well aware that with the return of his memories, he was gone from her forever. He would never be that man again. While she was glad for his re-found place in life, she would always mourn the loss of the man who had been hers — for a brief time, but a time she would never forget.

She stepped back to allow Leo to walk through the door in front of her, but he reached back and took her arm, and she realized then, while he would never admit it, not to her nor likely even to himself, that he needed her in that moment, even though it was his own family that he was facing.

He audibly breathed deeply, and then stepped through the door.

* * *

DAMN, but he was happy that Georgie was here. Somehow, her presence told him that everything was going to be all right.

Even when all of the evidence pointed otherwise.

"Leo! Oh, Leo!"

His mother was striding toward him now, her arms outstretched, and he felt Georgie melting away in the background as his mother, a woman who had hardly ever hugged him as a child, wrapped her arms around him. His sister trailed after her, standing just behind her, sniffling.

He stood still, shocked, as his mother took a moment to rest her head against his chest, then leaned back and lifted cool hands to cup his cheeks, the cold metal of her many rings striking against his skin.

"I can hardly believe it. We thought you were dead. For so long, Leopold. For so long."

"I understand, Mother, and I'm sorry. I truly am."

"You must tell us everything."

"I will tell you all that I can."

Which was true. He would say what he could say in front of Georgie and without placing any of them in danger.

"You gave us a dreadful scare, Leo," his sister scolded him as she wiped away a tear. Sarah smacked him on the shoulder before leaning in for a hug of her own.

"Son."

His father, tall and regal as ever, stood and held his hand out toward him. Leo took it, shaking it, knowing that this was the most emotion he would ever see from his father, although if he wasn't mistaken, was that the slightest sheen of tears covering his eyes? No, it couldn't be.

"I am glad to see you alive and well," his father continued. "I am also interested in hearing just how your family was put in such a difficult position."

Leo swallowed and nodded. No, there was definitely no sheen of tears. He should have known better. That was a glint of anger glimmering in his father's eyes — he just wasn't entirely sure who it was directed at.

"I understand, Father, and it will all make sense soon."

"I should hope so. Your brother most especially deserves an apology. They returned from Lyme Regis in wait for word of your return to us."

His brother, who Leo hadn't noticed until now, was standing near the sofa with his arm around a woman, who must be his new wife. She was beautiful, completely Perry's opposite in looks, her skin an umber-brown while Perry's was so pale they had teased him as children, her hair as black as his was fair.

Leo hoped that she was opposite him in countenance as well, for Perry needed someone to challenge him. Although if he had convinced his parents to allow him to marry a woman of his own choosing, then his little brother had obviously grown a bit of a backbone while Leo had been gone.

"Perry," he said, a true smile crossing his face as he crossed to his brother, not hesitating to fold a surprised Perry in his embrace. "Thank you for all you have done. And I'm sorry."

Perry nodded, although his gaze was troubled. "Much has happened while you were gone. I know you asked me to look after Anne, and I did, but she and I, well, that is, I met Rose, and—"

"There is nothing to concern yourself, over, Perry. Now, please introduce me to the wife I have heard so much about."

"Of course," Perry said with a grateful smile. "Leo, this is Rose."

Leo smiled, hoping to put her at ease, and was surprised when she reached out and clasped one of his hands within both of hers.

"I cannot tell you how happy we were to hear that you were still with us. We have been waiting to see you again."

She looked past him to the doorway.

"Thank you, Georgie."

Georgie said nothing, just nodded at the rest of them. Leo longed to reach out to her, to pull her in and have her join them in this moment instead of standing at the doorway like a stranger or a member of the staff, but it wasn't his place. Not now.

"Well, shall we?" he said, gesturing to the seating arrangements of the small parlor, and they all took a seat close to one another.

He took a breath, unsure of where to begin.

"What I am about to tell you must remain in this room, do you understand?"

They all agreed, but he had to be sure they understood.

Rose looked troubled, but she nodded and gripped Perry's hand, and Leo gave her a slight nod in return, appreciating her loyalty to the family.

He looked over at Sarah, whose head was down, staring at her hands which were twisting around one another. As though sensing his stare, she looked up, caught his gaze, and nodded her assent for him to tell her part of the story.

"There was an… incident just over a year ago. At Lord and Lady Alberta's ball. Sarah had taken a moment to herself, and she was cornered alone in a parlor by Lord Lovelace."

Their parents straightened, and turned to stare at Sarah.

117

"What were you doing alone?"

"I was—"

"That's beside the point," Leo interrupted, hearing the harsh strain of his words as he continued. "Lovelace took... liberties, despite Sarah's repeated denials."

"What?" His father stood upon his roar, beginning to pace the room. He turned to Sarah, raking a hand through his silver hair. His voice had lost its anger, but was now practically broken. "Why didn't you tell us?"

"I..." Sarah finally looked up, tears in her eyes. "I didn't know if anyone would believe me, that I didn't want any of it. He didn't... ruin me, but," she sniffed, her words nearly losing sound, coming out in a whisper. "It was awful."

"Sarah told me about it, but didn't tell me who it was for some time, as she knew nothing would come of it. That's when, Father, I spoke to you about pushing forward this bill, for I was enraged by the thought that a man could get away with such a thing. Then a few weeks later, I heard Lovelace bragging about it at The Red Lion. He didn't know I was there," Leo said, his words harsh. "When I found out it was him who attacked Sarah, I... I challenged him."

"To a duel?" Perry's eyes widened.

"Yes." Leo nodded his assent. "We met the next day at dawn."

"But who was your second?" Perry asked, his mouth agape.

"Billings."

"Billings? But he's been missing from London since... since..." Realization dawned upon Perry. "Since you left. He's been on the Continent, and hasn't returned. I heard his debts were all paid off, though."

"Makes sense," Leo muttered. "I don't know if I could have actually brought myself to kill Lovelace, even after what he had done. I remember aiming the pistol, but I must have hesitated. Things are a bit foggy. He shot and... well, I thought I was dead. Everything went black, and the next thing I remember, I was on a ship bound for New South Wales."

They all looked at him incredulously, and he scratched his head, aware of how far-fetched this must all sound, but needing them to understand the truth of it. He told them about the physician, about the manifest, about working his way home.

"Why didn't you write us?" Sarah asked, even as tears streamed down her face at his story.

Leo sighed. "I wasn't entirely sure what had happened to Lovelace or whether he thought me dead. I thought it best to try to keep you safe, to not tell you that I was alive until I could ascertain the danger of whether he might try to get to me through you. Then when the ship was about to enter the harbor, there was an explosion. For a time, all I could remember were events after that. I came to, floating on a piece of wood in the middle of the Thames. I smelled as though I was rotting myself, but I was alive, at least. When I washed onto shore, it was there that I met Geor—Miss Jenkins. She's a Bow Street detective," he explained to his parents, who nodded, apparently already knowing. He was surprised. They were becoming rather accepting in a few short months.

"At this point I had completely forgotten who I was, had lost all of my memories. One thing I did know, however, was that I was in danger, and that going anywhere that I might be recognized was a mistake."

"So what did you do?" Sarah asked, leaning forward, her elbows on her knees and the blue-green eyes that they all shared wide as she stared at him.

"I convinced her to take me elsewhere, to allow me to recover while she tried to determine who I was."

"And then?" Perry asked.

"I attended the Keswick masquerade to see if I might recognize anyone. However, Lovelace recognized me there, called me by my name. It sounds completely mad, I know, but it was enough to trigger my memories. The next morning I woke up and remembered who I was. I knew that I could not come home and put you all in any danger, but nor did I want to leave Miss Jenkins at risk any longer either. I disappeared, leaving her a note. She attended your wedding, Perry, where she then learned of my — Lord Richmond's — reappearance. She finally put it all together but didn't want to share my secrets until she knew it was safe and could talk to me. She was able to find me again and convinced me that I had to come speak to you all — and to Anne."

He finished, sitting back against the hard-backed chair that had obviously been carried in from the dining room.

His family all simply sat and stared at him in disbelief.

"That's quite a story," his father said, his voice gravelly.

"Yes," Leo agreed. "I know Lovelace is behind this, and he is working with Marbury, who was his second during the duel. I cannot accuse them of anything without evidence. Even then, if I attempt to get them tried for dueling, I am just as much at fault."

"You think they will try to kill you again?"

Leo shrugged. "They might. They went to great lengths to ensure I remained dead."

"Then kill them before they kill you."

They all turned as one to Sarah, who shrugged at their stares.

"What?" she said with a shrug, "it is the only way to ensure your safety."

"Georgie thinks that we should go about this through legal means. She just has to find enough evidence to convict them."

They looked at Georgie, who nodded.

"It is true, however," she said, her voice, one that provided a sure sense of calm, washing over the room, "that Leo could also be tried. As it is, the lords at fault will most likely claim privilege and nothing will come of it. You would, however, be free, Leo — I'm so sorry, Lord Richmond — as the truth would be in the open."

"But we could be scandalized," his mother said, and Georgie nodded.

"Perhaps. You would know more of such a thing than I."

"Is anyone else involved?" Rose asked, looking around to them. "It hardly seems to be something a man like this Lord Lovelace could do on his own."

"His second," Leo muttered. "Lord Marbury."

They all paused for a moment, realizing what — or who — they were up against.

"Well, Lord Richmond," Rose said, breaking the silence, but he interrupted.

"Call me Leo."

"Very well. Leo. Just what are you going to do now?"

A very good question.

"I—"

Before he could say anything, however, Collins stood at the door.

"Lady Montrose and Lady Anne Fitzgerald to see you, my lord."

CHAPTER 15

*L*eo's family filed out of the room — well, all except for Sarah, who stayed put on her corner of the sofa, staring away from them all and out the window, as though if she tried hard enough, they wouldn't notice her presence in the room.

Leo stood in wait for them to leave and for Lady Anne to enter. Georgie was the first out the door, and while she didn't turn around to look at him, Leo could read the tense set of her shoulders.

"Sarah," Leo's mother finally hissed, and Sarah had no choice but to look over, although she pouted when she saw her mother waving to the door. "Out."

She left, but Leo's mother stayed, standing just inside the door as Lady Montrose and Lady Anne walked in.

Anne smiled at him tremulously, nodding as she slightly curtseyed to him, while Lady Montrose looked at him in horror.

"My apologies on my attire," he said, looking down at himself. "Secrecy was of the utmost importance. I cannot share the entirety of what has occurred, but I am still concerned that there may be some danger."

"I... see," Lady Montrose said, her thin eyebrows rising so high that Leo was concerned they might disappear right into her hairline.

Anne recovered more quickly.

"I am so glad to see you well, my lord," she said, to which Leo nodded in return.

"And I must apologize for causing so much distress and confusion."

"I am sure it was not your fault."

"Even so."

It was only now he realized that in defending his own family's honor, he had put Anne's at risk. It was something he had never considered as he began to perceive just how selfish he had been prior to his unplanned exile. The air grew tense with the silence between them as they stood there, staring at one another.

Despite the fact he had regained his memories, Leo felt as though he was staring at a stranger. Had such formalness always existed between them? Perhaps they had never had a great love affair, but they *had* considered themselves in love.

Had they been so wrong? Did Anne still feel the same? And what would he do if she did?

"It is wonderful to see the two of you together again," Lady Montrose said, clasping her hands together. She was an older version of Anne, and evidence that Anne would most likely retain her innocent beauty throughout her life.

Only... it was a beauty that didn't call Leo. Not like the beauty of another.

"Lady Montrose, Mother, do you suppose that Lady Anne and I could have a moment alone?" he asked, raising a brow. "We will leave the door open."

The two matrons looked at one another as though

deciding together, before finally Lady Montrose turned to the pair of them and nodded. "Yes, if Anne's maid remains."

"Of course," Leo murmured, as Anne's maid nodded from her place in a chair near the window, where Leo hadn't even noticed her.

The women left the room, and Leo hoped that his mother would remind Lady Montrose just how important it was that they keep this meeting to themselves.

"Shall we?" he asked Anne, sweeping his arm out to the sitting area his family had just vacated, and she nodded shyly, taking a seat on the sofa while he chose a chair across from her. Her gloved hands were folded in her lap, her eyes upon them as she didn't lift her soft gaze to look at him, instead keeping whatever she was thinking and feeling within.

"Are you well, my lord?" she asked her gloves.

"I am," he said. "And I meant what I said, Anne. I truly am sorry to have caused you such distress. I can imagine how difficult it must have been to decide what to do with your life when your betrothed was presumed dead."

She nodded jerkily.

"At first, they wanted me to marry your brother, but I couldn't. Not when he was so in love with his Miss Ellis. Mrs. Belmont, I suppose I should say."

"It is fortunate it all worked out," he said, tapping his fingers upon his knee, unsure what else to say. "How are you feeling now... about *our* marriage?"

As they sat here awkwardly, all Leo could think about was what marriage would be like with Anne. He knew she was kind, would be dutiful, would never question him and would allow him to do as he pleased.

It was what he had always thought he had wanted.

Until now.

Until Georgie.

He was shocked to find that he rather *liked* being questioned, being challenged, being held accountable and asked to think in a different way. It didn't exactly make life any easier, but did it, perhaps, make life *better*? If he married Anne, he would always remain the same person, the man who didn't think of anyone but himself and his own class of people, who would never see the world or even wonder if there was another perspective he should be considering. That was every nobleman's dream, was it not?

But the past two months had proven otherwise. They had proven that, maybe, there was another path for him. The only problem was that he wasn't exactly free to take it.

"How do I feel about our marriage?" Anne finally lifted her face to him, and he was surprised to find she had gone quite pale. Her lower lip was trembling slightly while her light blue eyes were flicking back and forth from one side of the room to another.

"Anne, are you quite all right?"

He meant to ask the question kindly, but perhaps she needed a gentler hand.

For at his words, she burst into tears.

Leo sat frozen for a moment. Crying women were not exactly his speciality. Come to think of it, he had never seen Georgie actually cry. Her eyes had been brightened by a couple of unshed tears, but she had never allowed them exit.

He stood, his movements jerky as he walked over to take a seat beside Anne and awkwardly patted her on the shoulder.

"There, there," he said, but the words sounded empty even to his own ears. "Whatever is the matter?"

Fortunately her cries were soft, so he could only hope that they wouldn't bring their mothers running.

"It's just—" She sniffed, looking up at him, her blue eyes watering in earnest. "Oh, Leo, I am ever so sorry, but I just cannot marry you."

It took Leo a couple of seconds to register what she said. *Anne* didn't want to marry *him*?

"I do apologize, Lady Anne, if I have done anything to insult you or to cause you concern. I can assure you—"

"Oh, it's not that," she said, taking his proffered handkerchief and wiping her eyes as she began to pace the room. "It has nothing to do with you at all."

She took a deep breath, wringing her hands together as she turned back toward him, her eyes still watery but her sobs subsided.

"While you were gone," she said softly, "Lord Perry began to court me, as was expected by our families. One day, while out in your curricle—"

"*Perry* drove my curricle? With *my* horses?"

Leo had always had a passion for his horses and carriages. Perry, with his absent-mindedness, had *never* been allowed to drive them.

"As far as I know, it was just the once. Your father suggested it. Anyway, he fell out of the curricle—"

"He *what*?"

He loved his brother, but dear God, he would never understand him.

"And I was left with the runaway horses. A man rescued me and the pair. Mr. Clark. He is actually a partner at the stone factory that Rose's friend, Madeline Drake, owns."

Drake... the detective.

"Anyway, a few days later I went to thank Mr. Clark, and we... well..."

Her cheeks had turned bright red, but Leo wasn't sure just how extreme the situation had to be to cause Anne embarrassment.

"Oh, we quite enjoyed one another's company!" she burst out, breaking into the widest smile he had ever seen on her face. "So much so, that we began arranging to see one another whenever we can."

She exchanged a look with her maid, who was obviously involved in whatever deception Anne had required.

"Sometimes we meet at a book shop, sometimes while walking in Hyde Park. Sometimes I sneak away from a ball to meet him in the gardens. Oh! Nothing untoward."

She shook her hand in front of her, her eyes finally meeting Leo's, full of apology and sorrow. "You see, my lord, I have fallen in love with him. I thought I loved you, truly I did, and I know I should follow through on this betrothal, that to break it would be nothing but the worst sort of scandal, but I just... I just don't know how to live without Mr. Clark."

A joyous freedom exploded within Leo's chest as the weights that had been resting upon his shoulders flew off and crashed to the ground.

He stepped toward Anne, taking her hands within his.

"Lady Anne," he said, keeping his voice gentle, "you must not worry yourself. For I understand completely."

"You do?" The words were nearly breathless, and he nodded.

"I have found myself enraptured by another as well. However, I would never have left you to face such a scandal due to my contrary feelings."

"But that is exactly what I am doing to you."

"What we are doing to each other."

"Oh, dear," she said with a slight laugh as she placed a hand over her heart. "I can hardly believe this. I thought you would be most upset. I was so worried."

"I understand," Leo said with what he hoped was a gentle smile. "Now, we must determine just how we can break off this betrothal with as little scandal as possible. I would not wish to sully your name — although it sounds as though that might be changing soon, anyway."

Anne looked down against at her hands, which she had removed from Leo's grip.

"That is something I must discuss with you as well, Leo," she said, her fingers interlacing now. "I must ask you for a favor. It is a particularly large ask, in light of everything I have just told you."

"All right."

"My parents will most certainly not be pleased to learn about my fondness for Mr. Clark. He has done well for himself, yes, but he is still a merchant, and from rather humble beginnings. He is not at all what they would want for their daughter."

Leo could see that, with Anne being the daughter of a marquess.

"Would you mind awfully if we continue the charade of our betrothal until such time that Mr. Clark and I decide just how we can be together? We most likely will have to run away together, although I would prefer to have my parents' blessing. As you have asked for such secrecy of this meeting, I assume that we would not be expected to be out courting right now anyway."

"You are correct."

"Would you mind, then, awfully?"

So his name would be tied to hers for a while longer. Leo didn't see how that would pose any threat — after all, his heart and his intentions were now free to follow the path they longed to take — the path toward Georgie.

"No, Anne, I wouldn't mind at all. If there is anything you need from me to ensure your happiness, please tell me."

"Oh, thank you," she said, beaming now. "Thank you so much."

She smiled up at him, which he returned in honor of their secret agreement.

Which was how their mothers found them, both ladies walking in with extremely pleased smiles on their faces. Leo sighed as he wondered just how he would eventually break the news to his parents that he was not, in fact, going to marry Lady Anne. He considered for a moment just how they would respond to the woman he *would* choose — a Bow Street detective who had been born on the streets, whose mother was currently residing in Bedlam.

Somehow, he didn't see it going overly well.

But what could they possibly do? Cut him off? They couldn't change the fact that he was the heir.

His newfound excitement, however, flooded away as Georgie returned to the room. For at the sight of her, he remembered — that he was the very one she was fighting against, that if she ever learned the truth, she would never look at him again, let alone entertain the idea of marriage.

He set his chin, as he made a decision in that moment.

He was just going to have to make sure she never found out.

In the meantime, he would make her his.

He had to.

CHAPTER 16

*G*eorgie was bursting to know what had occurred in this room between Leo and Lady Anne. They both seemed so calm, so at peace as the Fitzgeralds took their leave, and she didn't miss the conspiratorial glance the two betrothed exchanged. Leo himself seemed particularly smug, although his words to his parents went against everything both he and Anne had told her regarding their feelings for one another.

"We shall plan the wedding for a month's time," he said, and any hope Georgie had held onto dropped from her stomach to the tips of her toes at his words. But why would she care? She hadn't really ever thought she had a chance with a man like Leo — not in any legitimate way. "Hopefully we can clear up this mess by then. Would that be sufficient?"

"Oh, just wonderful!" his mother said, clapping her hands together. "I can hardly wait. Lady Montrose and I will begin planning immediately."

"I expected nothing less," he said wryly, even as his father clapped a proud hand on Leo's shoulder, which slightly killed Georgie inside as she stood at the door like an outsider.

Hide the emotion, Georgie, she sternly told herself. It was how she had gotten through most of her life, and that wasn't about to change now.

She had known not to become attached, had convinced herself that this was only a job — now she just had to believe it.

For Leopold Belmont was going to be married to Lady Anne Fitzgerald, and she was going to have to accept it.

"Remember, please don't share with anyone that I've returned," Leo instructed them before he left. "If anyone has questions about the wedding planning, tell them that you have received word of my survival, that I am to return by the wedding date, but that you have not yet seen me. I don't want anyone assuming that I am here."

"Do you not think this is all slightly ludicrous?" his mother asked, lifting her brows with a glance over at Georgie, as though it was all her fault. "I can hardly believe that Lord Lovelace would come after you once more."

"I wouldn't put it past him to send someone to try again, and I do not want to put anyone in harm's way. We've probably already stayed too long."

"Where are you staying, son?" his father asked, but Leo shook his head. "I cannot say."

"Very well," his father said with a sigh, although he didn't seem particularly pleased. "How should I contact you if I need to find you?"

"You can send a message to Bow Street, my lord," Georgie said, stepping forward. "I can locate your son for you."

Lord Sheriden looked her up and down as though assessing her competence before finally nodding. "Very well," he said dryly, then turned to Leo one last time. "It was good to see you."

And with that, Georgie and Leo took their leave, back through the servants' entrance.

"How do you feel?" Georgie asked once they were back on the road, walking toward home — her home.

"What do you mean?" His jaw was clenched tightly, and Georgie realized he was just as adept as she was at hiding his true emotions, although his necessity for doing so was for altogether different reasons. She had to do so to stay alive. He had to because that was what he had always been taught.

"I mean, were you happy to see your family again? Lady Anne?"

Georgie was very proud of herself that her voice did not break as she asked the question.

"I am glad that they no longer have to assume me dead," he said, then released a low chuckle. "I think Perry was relieved more than anything. He would have hated becoming the earl with everything within him."

"I think he was also happy to discover that his brother is alive."

Did these noble families ever actually allow any emotion into their relationships?

"That may be so as well," he admitted.

"Lady Anne must have been so pleased." She hoped her words sounded nonchalant.

Leo snuck a look at her, as though to assess her true feelings.

She simply waited for his answer.

"Actually... that was a bit of a surprise as well."

"Oh?"

Even as she held her tongue, her heartbeat started to quicken as much as Georgie commanded it to resume its usual pace.

"Yes... it seems she has fallen in love with another."

Georgie was silent for a moment, her eyes on the ground, for she couldn't look at Leo, didn't want to see what his reaction might be. "That must have been hard for you to hear."

"You know what?"

He paused, and she realized he was waiting for her to look up at him. She did so, shocked by the intensity of his gaze.

"What's that?"

"I was glad of it." His words were heavy with relief, and with something else that she couldn't quite place — until she saw the heat in his eyes, the desire radiating from them with the same intensity that was dripping off his words.

"You were?" she squeaked. Damn it. She didn't squeak.

"I was," he said, slowly, reaching between them and, ever so softly, stroking one of her fingers, with just enough of a touch that it sent shivers down her spine.

"But... but you were talking about the wedding with your family. Is that still continuing?"

"The charade of planning it is continuing, yes," he said with a nod, dropping her finger as with her question she had broken the moment between them. "Anne would like to marry this merchant of hers but she does not think her parents will allow it. She asked that we continue to plan the wedding in order to provide her with more time to determine what they will do."

"You don't mind?"

"That she wants to marry another? No. I just hope that we can sort out all of these messes in time."

"Well, that's what I'm here for," she said with forced cheer, just as they arrived back at her rooms. "I have also spoken with Drake and he has agreed to help. He will meet with us tomorrow."

Leo grunted slightly as his expression cleared. "Drake. The officer. Fine, if you insist. Although I do think the less people that know of this, the better."

"He can help. I know he can. As for the rest of the day, I think, perhaps, we should discuss all of the possibilities of just who else would hold a grudge against you, who would be agreeable to work with Lovelace, who would have enough reason to threaten a lord. Your enemies, anything that you might be involved in that would cause someone to harbour ill will toward you. There was mention of people who might have reason to not be pleased with you? Why would that be? Why would your death be beneficial to th—ooh!"

Georgie's thoughts came to an abrupt halt when they stepped through the door into her rooms, for as soon as it was shut behind them, Leo picked her up, spun her around, and slammed her against the back of the door, cushioning the impact with his arm.

Before she could say a word, his lips were crushing hers, stealing every word, every thought, with each caress of his lips and sweep of his tongue.

The kiss was magic. *He* was magic. This... was everything she had been waiting for and yet was trying to tell herself she didn't want, didn't need. For this was but a fleeting moment, one that was the result of the yearning they had held for one another for weeks now. When it was satisfied, what then? He would move on, perhaps not to marry Anne, but another woman just like her. Where would that leave Georgie?

All of the questions swirled around her mind, only the more he kissed her, the more muddled they became — a state Georgie had never found herself in, for she preferred to be alert, attuned to everything around her.

Which was interesting, for, as confused as her thoughts were, the rest of her senses were heightened. She was filled with Leo's scent, a musky masculine laced with coffee and cinnamon. His biceps were hard beneath her fingers, inviting her to sink her grasp more deeply into them. His muscled thigh fit between her legs, and she was tempted to rub herself against it, to find the pleasure he offered her.

She wrapped her arms around his neck, knowing she

should be using them to push him away, but finding instead that all she seemed to be capable of doing at the moment was drawing him closer. For the truth was, as much as she knew this was a mistake, that nothing good could come of this — she didn't really care.

* * *

LEO HAD ALWAYS IMAGINED JUST how sweet Georgie would be if he had the chance to truly taste her. He had kissed her before but this... this was different.

He hadn't been prepared for her spiciness. She kissed him with the same abandon as when she laughed — long and unabashedly. Everything he gave, she returned in equal measure, and he had never been so completely overtaken by a woman as he was her.

The way she moaned when his tongue plundered her mouth. The way she arched her back to more fully press against him, or rubbed against his thigh. The way she twined her fingers into his hair, forcing his head down toward her so that he could more thoroughly capture her mouth.

Every inch of her was fire, and she had completely engulfed him in her flame.

He had thought he would never be free to lose himself in her, that he was promised to another and would have to mollify himself with memories and imaginings of her for the rest of his days.

But when Anne had released him from his promise, it was no longer just wishful thoughts that filled his head, but possibilities — of what he and Georgie could be to one another, what he could do for her, what they could mean for one another.

He knew he probably should have discussed this with her before attacking her like a man possessed.

But that was what he currently was, and he had acted accordingly. He could only be grateful that she hadn't pushed him away, hadn't opened the door and led him out through it, hadn't told him that she never wanted to see him again.

Deep within him, however, he had been aware that she would never do such a thing. For he could sense that she wanted him with just as much abandon as he wanted her.

She pushed away from the door, taking him with her as she reached up and gripped the lapels of his gaudy jacket, pulling them down with such strength that she nearly wrenched out his shoulder. He pulled the sleeves free for her and she finished the job, dispensing of the garment entirely. He yearned for her with a desperation he had never felt before, and he picked her up, setting her atop the table which was pushed against the wall.

She moaned into his mouth as he stood between her legs, pressing himself against her, while she wrapped thighs around him, drawing him ever closer.

He ran his hands up and down her sides, even as he rocked with her, both welcoming and trying to be rid of the fantasy in his mind of her laid out on the table before him.

"We shouldn't be doing this," he said, breaking his mouth away from hers but not leaving her, touching his forehead to hers as he panted against her.

"No," she said, shaking her head. "We shouldn't."

"But why… why not?" he couldn't stop himself from asking, even though he knew very well why not. It was just that he was no longer thinking with his head.

But Georgie was.

"Because… you and I are not going to end up together. We both know that. This is… temporary."

"Does it have to be?" he asked, looking into those hauntingly beautiful brown eyes. "I want you, Georgie, with every part of me. I have ever since I first laid eyes on you, even when you were a blurry haze in front of me. Ever since I heard your voice, saw your face, which I thought was that of an angel. And now that I am free? Maybe this was all meant to be."

As long as she would accept him for who he was and what he had done. That was still to be answered.

He knew, however, deep within him, that he could not have her, not like this. Not with such lies and unspoken truths between them. But nor could he bring himself to share with her that he was the force she was fighting against.

She didn't answer him with words, but instead wrapped her hands around the back of his head and pulled him to her once more, kissing him with all of the growing need that he felt within himself. He knew he couldn't have her... but that didn't mean he couldn't give her all of the passion and pleasure she deserved.

He trailed his fingers up from her ankle to knee to thigh, tugging her clothing up and away from her, until she was bare before him. When he brushed against the juncture between her legs, she moaned and gripped his hair so hard that she pulled at it, and he had never felt such pleasure within pain.

He left her lips, kissing his way up her neck, her collarbone, to find the soft skin of her earlobe, before he trailed his way back down, going lower this time, pulling down her shirt to find the top swell of her breasts.

He ran a finger against her folds, finding her wet, ready, and he nearly lost all restraint and rid himself of his breeches right then and there. He wrested control of himself in time and when she dropped down to her elbows and leaned back, moaning his name, he couldn't help himself from bending down and capturing that nipple in his mouth, flicking his tongue over it as he used his fingers between her legs, playing at her entrance while rubbing her most sensitive of places. He moved to the other breast and when she pushed her hips against him, he responded, pumping his fingers in and out as his thumb circled her and he returned his lips to hers, his tongue plundering her mouth in time with his fingers.

She suddenly went tight around him as she threw her head back, nearly rigid as she cried aloud her release, until she collapsed against him and he caught her to him, picking her up as he carried her back to the bedroom.

"I can— I can walk you know," was the first thing she said, and he smirked.

"I know."

"I'm kind of heavy."

"Are you questioning my strength?"

"No."

"Enough out of you then."

She stared at him in shock as he tossed her onto the bed, before he jumped onto it and joined her.

"You know..." she said, beginning to trail her fingers along the edge of his trousers, and he sucked in a breath.

"What's that?"

"I was thinking I— did you hear that?" she asked, lifting her head, suddenly alert.

"Hear what?"

A knock. Now he heard it. There was definitely a knock.

"Damn it!" he muttered. He did not intend to fully take her, but he had imagined them having a bit more fun together.

"Yep, that's a knock."

"Georgie? Are you in there?"

"He'll go away," Leo mumbled, even as he turned over and placed a hand on his forehead, knowing full well that he was beaten by whoever was on the other side of that door.

"It's Drake," she said, shrugging with some apology. "He knows we're here."

"Best let him in," Leo said, even as every part of him — one part in particular — ached fiercely. For her.

That would have to be remedied later, however. For now, apparently, they were back to the business matters at hand.

CHAPTER 17

This was one of those times when Georgie was particularly grateful that it didn't take her much time nor effort to prepare herself. She quickly threw on a chemise with a plain navy dress overtop, before wrapping her curls into a braid. She took a quick glance in the mirror to assure herself that she did not look completely ravished before she went out to answer the knock, closing the bedroom door behind her as she went, as Leo was still lacing up his breeches.

"Drake, good to see you," she said, opening the door, and he nodded, looking her over as though he guessed something was amiss, although he respected her enough not to say anything.

"I'm sorry to come today unexpectedly. I had nothing else to occupy my time with, however, so I thought it was best to come speak to you and your lord as soon as I could."

"He's not *my* lord," Georgie said, her cheeks warming, and Drake snorted.

"You haven't said anything to Madeline, have you?" she asked.

"No, of course not," Drake said. "This is business."

Well, part of it was business. The part that she was going to share with Drake.

She and Drake had become fast friends since they had both joined Bow Street a few years ago. There had never been anything romantic between them, as they found themselves drawn to one another in their shared pursuit of justice as well as the loss of their parents from their lives at a young age. Georgie had only met Drake's wife, Madeline, when he had asked her to watch over her when she had been in danger last year. Georgie found that she rather enjoyed the company of the woman who looked as frail as could be but held a rigid strength within her.

But Drake was still her closest confidant, and she trusted him to keep her secrets — which meant to keep Leo's as well.

"Where is the nob?"

"Drake!"

"I'm sorry. Where is *Lord Richmond*?"

"He had to change garments, so he is using my bedroom."

"I see."

"You see what?"

"Nothing."

His amused expression said otherwise, but thankfully, he left it alone.

"Drake."

They both turned at the sound of the deep bass voice that emanated from the door of Georgie's bedroom, which Leo thankfully had already closed behind him. No need for Drake to see any evidence that would cause him to suspect anything further.

"Richmond." Drake crossed the room and shook Leo's hand. "Georgie has told me your story and I am well acquainted with your brother now. Why don't we have a brief discussion and see if we can't help you determine how we might put an end to all of this so that you can find your way home?"

Home. Where, once Leo returned, Georgie would likely never see him again. But that was beside the point.

Leo nodded uncomfortably, although why, Georgie had no idea.

"I'm sure I won't be asking anything Georgie hasn't already," Drake said as he took a seat on Georgie's worn sofa. She sat beside him as Leo took a chair.

"You and Lord Lovelace fought a duel, which he won, correct?"

Leo's expression turned stony.

"I suppose you could say that."

"So instead of admitting to the duel, Lovelace tried to have your body hidden?"

"That's right. I don't know who actually did it for him, but I ended up on the transport ship instead. They arranged to have another body 'found' as mine, beaten too badly to be sure of its identity, but apparently witnesses told them that it was me."

"And you believe Lovelace is going to try to have you killed again?"

"If I'm not here to tell tales, then what could possibly happen to him? My second was paid off and, knowing Billings and his dealings, was likely blackmailed. I doubt we'll hear from him again soon. Then there was the incident with my sister. No one would believe her, but they might believe me. I don't think that Lovelace — nor his second, Marbury — will try anything himself. He'll have someone else do it, although from what I hear, he is in dun territory so I'm not sure who he is hiring or how he would do such a thing."

"Is there anything else you're involved in that might be of concern?" Georgie asked, to which Leo shook his head quickly.

"No, of course not," he said, and Georgie narrowed her eyes at the obvious lie.

Drake looked between them, sensing some tension, before continuing.

"Tell me what someone might hold against you. Any clubs, organizations that someone might have issue with?"

"Just the usual," Leo said with a shrug. "White's, Tattersalls, nothing out of the ordinary."

"What of any women?" Drake asked, even as Georgie's stomach tightened while she prepared for the response. "Were you involved with one that another gentleman might have issue with? Any man's wife or intended?"

"No."

"Does anyone owe you money?" Georgie said. "Were you —are you—a gambler?"

"Nothing serious," Leo replied, scratching his forehead, and Georgie leaned in, sensing there was something he was hiding, something that could help them if only he would let them.

"Do *you* owe anyone money?" Georgie asked, becoming rather impatient now, wanting to reach out and shake the answers from him, but knowing that wouldn't exactly help their cause.

"Of course not," he repeated with such disdain, that she immediately believed him.

Despite Drake's completely neutral countenance, Georgie knew he sensed the answers hidden there just as much as she did.

"What is the issue, then, Leo?" she asked, staring at him so intently that he eventually broke her gaze. "What aren't you telling us?"

"Georgie," Drake murmured, tapping her knee quickly, enough of a signal to tell her that she was becoming too emotionally involved. She sat back abruptly. She knew, as a

143

woman, one of the greatest protests to her involvement with Bow Street was that she would allow her emotion to get the best of her, to cloud her judgement and cause her to act rashly.

With her actions right now, she was only proving all of the naysayers right. Thank goodness it was just Drake here.

"She is right, though," Drake said, tilting his head to the side. "We can't help you if you don't provide us more answers."

"Do you worry about Sarah?" Georgie asked. "That Lovelace might try anything else with her?"

Leo shook his head. "He would have done something by now. And Sarah is engaged to be married. She has Sherwater, who will look after her now."

"When you were in Lovelace's study, you found the note about the body, and the diary from last year does put him at the club with you on the night you disappeared. That is something, but I'm not sure that it's enough," Drake said, crossing his arms over his chest. "I'll look into Lovelace, see if I can gather any more information on him — or on Marbury, who could be another key to this. Lord Richmond, if you think of anything else that can help, be sure to let us know."

"Of course," Leo murmured, "and thank you."

Georgie followed Drake to the door, bid him farewell, and then turned to look at Leo, crossing her arms over her chest.

"What are you not saying?"

"Pardon me?"

"You're hiding something," she said, shaking her head. "I can tell. Out with it,"

"Nothing at all."

She grunted in frustration, turning away from him even

as he lifted his hands to her arms. She had no desire to lose herself in his touch, not when she needed to focus.

"I am going to go out to check in at Bow Street," she said. "I need you to remain here. When you are ready to tell me just what you are hiding, please do and then I can actually do something about this investigation."

"Georgie—"

"I'll see you shortly."

Then she shrugged into her cloak, and shut the door on him.

LEO STARED after Georgie with frustration. He wanted to tell her. Truly. He wanted to share with her all of his thoughts, all of his frustrations.

But he knew that if he told her that his father was the one who had put the bill forward at his own urging, determined to see harsher sentences for criminals, she would leave him forever. He had only seen one side of the argument, had never considered the criminals as, well, as people.

He sat back in his chair, the thoughts rolling within him. He didn't want to see a woman like Georgie's mother face harsher penalties, he truly didn't. Now, especially that he had seen the conditions she lived in, he knew that it would be wrong to expect that she should have to suffer any more.

He could see what Georgie was saying. Some people committed crimes because they saw no other option for survival, while others... he thought of Lovelace, who had treated Sarah as he had, or people who were truly guilty of the worst crimes and yet practically got away with it... it caused his blood to boil. He had been so intent on revenge against Lovelace that he hadn't considered all of the people who actually fell within the trappings of the system.

He began to pace the room, but it felt to him like the walls were closing in on him, that these friendly rooms that called to him with such a feeling of home were suddenly his enemy, threatening to capture him like a fly in a spiderweb.

He had to get out.

He donned his most gaudy borrowed clothes and shoved a cap low over his head, hoping he looked like any fisherman or dock worker, and let himself out of Georgie's rooms. She had given him a key, which he took while ignoring her strict instructions to stay put.

It wasn't as though he was being held captive. If he needed a walk, he needed a walk. He doubted anyone was waiting and watching for him. It wasn't as though Georgie's presence was what had kept anyone from approaching him.

He shoved his hands into his pockets as his pinched, borrowed boots hit the cobblestones. He hadn't gone far when a hand clapped his shoulder, and he whirled around, fists clenched, ready to defend himself.

"Ho, hold on a minute there, Gentleman Jackson!" It was the doctor, his hands held up in front of him in defense. "I'm sorry, I didn't mean to startle you. Just thought I saw you coming out of Georgie's. Didn't realize you were still around." The man eyed him with warranted suspicion.

"Yes," Leo said with a nod. "Georgie has been kind enough to allow me to stay while we... sort things out."

"Still don't have your memories?" The doctor asked, spinning his finger to tell Leo to turn around. He removed his cap for him, crouching over to look at the gash at the back.

"Actually, they did return," Leo said, bending so the slightly shorter man could take a look.

Carter grunted. "Georgie did a good job keeping you well, I see. She's a good girl, that one. If you know who you are, why are you still around?"

"It's a complicated matter," Leo began, cringing slightly as

146

he wasn't entirely sure where to begin. "I don't want to put anyone in danger — my family, nor Georgie. I left, but she was relentless. She found me and insisted that I return, at least until we can figure this out."

"Ah, so this was no accidental knock on the head."

"Not entirely," he said, uninterested in going over the entire story once more.

The doctor nodded slowly. "I know you likely don't mean Georgie any harm, but she won't ask this for herself, so I will ask for her. Be careful with her. Don't hurt her, intentionally or not. Even by staying here you are putting her reputation at risk. Unless you plan to do right by her?"

"I—" Leo scratched his head before placing the cap back upon it. "I don't really know yet what our future holds."

The doctor nodded. "Just think on what I said."

"Of course," Leo murmured. His first instinct had been to defend himself, to tell this doctor exactly what he thought of his veiled threats, but he quickly thought better of it. Carter was only trying to protect Georgie, and if anything, Leo should be glad that she had someone watching out for her.

The worst part was that Carter was right and Leo knew it.

Perhaps the best thing to do was to go talk to his father — without Georgie's presence — and decide just what they were going to do about this bill, if anything.

"Thank you again, Carter."

Leo stretched out his hand, passing Carter the coin he was owed. The doctor hesitated a moment before taking it, then tipped his hat at Leo before continuing along, toward St. Paul's in the distance.

Leo sighed as he turned to face in the direction of Mayfair. He hadn't gotten far, however, when he was grabbed by the shoulder once again. He turned around, ready to tell the doctor, Georgie's protector or not, exactly what he thought, when a beefy arm wrapped around his neck and began to drag him backward.

"Oh, for fu—" Leo tried to grunt, but found that his windpipe was too restricted for him to actually say anything. He kicked backward, catching the man in the shin, providing himself a brief respite. The man didn't release his grip, but he did loosen it enough that Leo was able to catch a quick breath. But then the arm tightened once more, and when Leo sent his elbow flying backward to connect with the man's gut, it was caught by another man who had appeared from beside them.

"Enough of that," he grunted, and the pair of them dragged him into a narrow alley between buildings, even as Leo desperately wondered just why no one had come to his aid. Although, would he have done so for a man he didn't know, putting himself in such danger? He wasn't sure. He'd like to think so, but he was beginning to question everything about himself.

"Let him go," the second man commanded, and as Leo turned around, ready to fight, he found his first attacker holding a knife.

"I'd put those fists away if I were you," he growled, his voice low and raspy, as though it was coated in a layer of smoke. Leo weighed his options, but before he could take a swing, a thick piece of rope came around his neck, the other man tightening the noose.

"There, there," came a singsong voice in his ear. "Just like having a little sleep."

Leo tried to fight it as the tightness of the rope increased, but black spots began to appear in front of his eyes. If only he had told Georgie how he really felt, he despaired as he began to completely lose all consciousness. If only—

Then suddenly the rope fell to the ground, with Leo following after it.

CHAPTER 18

*G*eorgie's heart was on the ground along with Leo, but at the moment, she didn't have a chance to stop and make sure he was alive. She was too busy taking care of the men who had tried to kill him.

Thank goodness Marshall had insisted on accompanying her back home. When she had arrived at Bow Street, he had all sorts of questions about where she had been and what happened to her "friend." Georgie had tried to stave off his questions, but Marshall had insisted on accompanying her home to determine just why Leo had become so settled in. Georgie didn't have the heart to tell him that she had already involved Drake in the case. She didn't want to insult Marshall, but Drake was much more level-headed about this kind of thing — and he didn't ask questions.

After stopping for a moment when they saw Carson, they had just turned onto Fleet Street when they heard a cry and saw the commotion. It didn't take them long to determine just what was happening on the side of the cobblestone street.

Georgie had tackled the man holding Leo with the

ferocity of a cat, hooking her arm around his neck as she jabbed him in the side, causing him to release Leo. Meanwhile, Marshall had swung one of his meaty fists into the face of the second attacker. Georgie quickly punched her foe in the kidney and while he was bent over, she lifted her knee to his chin.

Soon they had both men on the ground, and while Marshall tied their hands behind their backs with the very rope they had tried to kill Leo with, Georgie went to Leo, where he was now on his hands and knees, breathing heavily as he rubbed his throat.

"Let me see that," Georgie murmured, gently tipping his head back as she ran her ungloved fingers over his neck. The mark was red and raw, but he would survive.

She sat back on her heels and looked up at him from beneath her cap.

"I cannot leave you alone for a minute, can I?"

Leo lifted one corner of his lips sheepishly. "I honestly didn't think anyone would know who I was."

"No? Then why did Carson tell me he had just seen you?"

"I—" Leo lifted his hands out to the side. "You're not my keeper, Georgie."

"No," she said, fixing him with a stare. "You're right. I am not."

She stood abruptly, having no wish to discuss this with him any further. There would be more than enough time for that later. She crossed to the men, where Marshall had propped them up against the wall.

"Who are you?" she demanded. "And what do you want with this man?" She pointed back toward Leo.

The one man laughed at her, despite the tooth that was now sticking out at an odd angle, a drop of blood sliding down his chin below it. "What do you care about a nob like 'im?"

Georgie picked up the knife he had dropped during the commotion, and slowly, not breaking eye contact with the man, lifted it up underneath his chin.

"Let's try this again, shall we?" she asked, hoping the glint in her eyes would scare him. "Tell me what you want with this man."

The man looked down at the knife Georgie held and swallowed, his neck bobbing as he did so.

"Georgie," Leo said from his place on the ground. "Just leave it."

The man looked sideways at Leo. "W-we were hired."

"By who?"

"I can't tell—fine, fine! I'll tell you. But I don't know his name."

"No?"

"He was a nob, that much I know."

Georgie looked back at Leo, finding that he was listening to them intently. "How did you know that?"

"He was dressed all fancy-like, and he spoke in that way they have, you know what I mean?"

"I do. Where did he find you? What did he ask you to do?"

"Don't tell them anything, Tub!"

"Tub?" Georgie raised an eyebrow. "I suggest you ignore your friend over there."

Tub looked from his partner to Georgie and back to his partner again before sighing and closing his eyes.

"He asked us to kill 'im."

"That much I gathered. Why?"

"I don't know!" the man cried, and by the wildness in his eyes, Georgie was inclined to believe him. "He gave us half the money up front, said we'd get the rest when there was proof of a body. Of 'is actual body. That part he added the second time, as we failed the first time through."

"So you were the men who put him on the transport ship?"

The man nodded morosely, even as the other man muttered curses under his breath, shaking his head in disappointment.

"Could hardly believe it when the nob showed up again saying the man had been resurrected. I don't know how it was possible, thought for sure he would've died from the wound. It was right nasty, it was. Didn't want to be the one guilty for his death, but if he happened to die—"

"I'm far too stubborn," Leo cut in dryly.

"If you don't know his name, tell me what the man looked like," Georgie demanded, and the two men share an expression.

"He looked like a nob," Tub said. "They all look the same."

"Hair color? Height? Build?" Georgie urged, and Tub looked down as he rubbed his head.

"Dark hair I think, but it was night. A little shorter than this one here," he said, nodding at Leo. "Thin. Carried himself like a dainty miss. That's 'ow I first knew he was a nob."

"Marbury," Leo grunted. "Lovelace's second."

Georgie nodded, though she wondered if the word of these men would be enough. Likely not.

"Very well. We'll take these men to Bow Street and then I'll return," she said to Leo, then eyed him steadily. "Do you think you can actually stay put this time?"

Leo nodded. "I can."

"Good," Georgie said with a set jaw. "I shall see you shortly."

* * *

Leo had other plans in mind, however.

152

If these men had found him here, then he knew it would only be a matter of time until he was discovered again. He was no longer going to run around like a scared mouse. He was going to do what he should have done a long time ago — face this like the nobleman he was.

He knew better this time than to leave with just a note. Instead, while Georgie was gone, he packed his few meagre belongings, folding everything else into a neat pile and cleaning up his bed space near the fireplace.

He knew he owed Georgie the truth, but he had no idea what she would think of him once he had shared all.

He tapped his knuckles upon the table, remembering all they had done there just the night before. How could so much change in just a few hours? He wondered as he placed his forehead down upon the table.

Which was how Georgie found him when she walked in a few minutes later.

"Leo?" she asked, her footsteps loud as she ran toward him. "Are you all right? I never should have left, I—"

"I'm fine," he said, rising slowly, still a little dizzy, but he waved a hand in front of his face. "I'm sorry, I didn't mean to worry you."

"Oh, thank goodness," she said as she took a seat next to him. "Well, at least the two that tried to do you in are no longer a problem."

"For now," he mused, and she eyed him curiously.

"What does that mean?"

"I suppose it means that we shall see whether anything actually comes of their punishment," he said. "Sometimes nothing does."

"I would be inclined to disagree with that," she said, frowning, a line forming between her eyes.

"I understand," he said, and he did, much more now than he ever would have previously. "Georgie."

He'd had an entire speech prepared, but after saying her name he found that he was arrested for a moment by her eyes, which met his just long enough for her to realize something else entirely. She looked to the bag at his feet.

"You're leaving."

"Yes, I—"

"You know that just because you were attacked again does not necessarily put me in immediate danger."

"I am a lord, for goodness sake, a future earl!" His declaration was accompanied with his abrupt standing, sending his chair crashing to the floor behind him and she flinched, but didn't back down.

"I realize that," she said cryptically.

"I shouldn't be hiding in some woman's rooms, peeking out from behind her skirts to see if it is safe to come out."

He hadn't realized how upset he was until he started talking, but now that he had loosed the words, it seemed he had lost all ability to rein them back in.

She made it worse by answering him as calmly as ever.

"I know that most men have difficulty when a woman comes to their rescue," she said. "That is one of the reasons I dress the way I do — so that it is not as obvious who I am."

"Oh, it's obvious," he said, a finger in the air now, as he picked up his tiny satchel and strode to the door. "I have to go. For more reasons than I care to discuss." He rubbed his forehead, aware that he was being a complete ass, but unable to stop himself. "I'm sorry, Georgie, I am. And I thank you for everything you have done for me. I will not be going home, but will be seeing if I can find suites at the Albany or a like establishment. Now that my family knows I am alive, I am sure they will be willing to pay for such."

"You are decided, then?" she said, standing stiffly, her arms crossed in front of her.

"Yes, I am," he said, telling himself just to walk out the

door without prolonging the goodbye, yet unable to move his feet from the ground. "When all this is settled, Georgie, then—"

"Then?"

She lifted an eyebrow mockingly, as though knowing that he could not say the words he was suggesting.

"Then perhaps we can make one another's acquaintance again."

"Unless you allow yourself to be killed."

"It's as I said, Georgie. I cannot hide any longer — especially behind you. If the only way to make these bastards come out is to emerge from hiding myself, then so be it. I will be ready and waiting for them."

"With what protection?"

"I may have been caught unawares before," he said gruffly, "but I will not allow that to happen again. I will be ready this time."

"Very well," she said with a shrug of one shoulder, although the tense set of her back told him far more than her nonchalant words did. "If you want to get yourself killed, it is no business of mine. Goodbye, Leo."

She held her chin high, and he wondered just how much she actually cared that he was leaving.

"Goodbye, Georgie," he said, walking out the door and shutting it softly behind him, even as he felt like he was going to be sick all over the pavement at his feet.

The worst of it was, he hadn't even told her the entirety of the truth.

Damn it, he should have just left a note.

CHAPTER 19

"*W*ell, Marshall, what's the latest?"

Marshall swiveled in his chair as Georgie dropped down into the one behind him.

"Oh, look who it is!" he said with a knowing smile. "I was wondering if you were ever going to return to us for more than a quick hello or if you had forever abandoned us for the case of the lost duke."

She rolled her eyes at him.

"He's not a duke. He's a viscount. A future earl."

"Ah, yes, that's right," Marshall said, tapping a finger against his temple. "How could I forget?"

"Well, it doesn't matter any longer. He's decided to return to his life, consequences be damned."

Marshall raised an eyebrow. "Did the two of you find yourselves in a lover's quarrel?"

"We are not lovers," she said with a glare his way.

Well, not exactly.

"So you are dropping the case, just like that?"

"I tried to look into it more yesterday, but didn't get very far. Lord Marbury is equally as involved, and it's difficult to find out much about the nobility when you're not from within. I'm going to have to recruit Alice."

Drake walked in then, though, unlike Marshall, he said nothing about her presence. Instead, he sat down with them and went straight to the topic on his thoughts.

"Georgie, sorry it's been more than the day I promised."

"Not a problem."

"I told you and Richmond that I would look into Lovelace and Marbury, and I—"

"What's that now?" Marshall leaned in between them, his thick red mustache filling Georgie's vision. He turned it now toward Georgie. "Did you ask *Drake* to help you with this?"

"Er—yes, but only because—"

"Well," Marshall huffed, crossing his arms over his chest as he turned around away from them. "After all I've done for you. I rescind my dinner invitation!"

Georgie held a hand in front of her face as she tried not to laugh. "Marshall, you never invited me. Your wife did."

"Then I revoke her invitation," he said stubbornly.

"You know you could never do that without catching her ire, which is something you would never, ever do," Georgie said, doing her best to keep her voice steady and even so as to not further insult Marshall.

"Of course I wouldn't," he said and then paused. "Very well, you can still come. But that doesn't mean that I'm happy about this."

"I know and I'm sorry, Marshall," Georgie tried again. "It's just Drake has a bit more access to that world, and—"

Marshall lifted a hand to stop her. "Say no more. I understand."

"All right, then," Georgie said, exchanging an amused glance with Drake. "Tell us, then, Drake, what have you found?"

"Lovelace and Marbury are both in a bit of debt, and

there have been accusations against Lovelace before. He has never actually been charged with anything."

"Of course not," she muttered, "not with him being a peer and all."

"Lady Sarah never accused him of anything either."

"No, she likely wouldn't. Perhaps if she was a man, but no one else saw it, and I'm sure it would only have harmed her reputation. Which is ridiculous."

"I agree with you," said Drake.

Georgie shook her head at the injustice.

"As for the men from yesterday," Drake said, lifting his hands in some confusion, "They must be connected, but so far we have nothing to tie those men to Lovelace besides the note you found."

"Marshall told you of the attack?" Georgie asked, nodding to the redheaded man's back.

"He did," Drake confirmed. "Did Richmond recall or tell you anything else that might help us?"

"Not really," Georgie said, shaking her head, "but I can tell he's hiding something. However, none of it matters anymore. For he's decided that he is no longer going to hide, but instead take rooms in a more public place and draw out his attacker."

"Oh?" Drake said, leaning back and steepling his fingers together. "That's an interesting strategy."

"It's stupid."

Drake shrugged. "I understand it, though. He strikes me as a man of action. To do nothing would be difficult."

"He could get himself killed."

"He could," Drake agreed with a nod. "But that's his own choice."

Georgie sighed as she dipped her pen in the inkwell and began scribbling on the page in front of her. "He did mention something interesting yesterday."

"Oh?"

"When his attacker described the gentleman who had hired him, he thought he recognized him as Lord Marbury."

"It makes sense," Drake said, looking off into the distance. "We need to learn more about him. There isn't much information available to me."

"He's cousin to Lady Anne. However, perhaps Alice would speak to her sister-in-law's friend for us. She's always run in those circles."

"Lady Dorrington?"

"Yes. Alice calls her Freddie."

"She might know, that's a good thought," Drake said with a nod. "Very well. We'll follow up on that and see what we can find."

"But after that, we're done with this," Georgie said, attempting to keep the bitterness from her tone. "If Le—Lord Richmond doesn't want us involved, then so be it."

Drake eyed her thoughtfully. "It's not like you to give up so easily."

"I'm not giving up. I just don't want to waste my time where it's not wanted."

"Very well," Drake said. "You're the boss."

"She's not our boss," Marshall said, clearly still listening to their conversation.

"You're a married man, Marshall," Drake said, shaking his head. "You'd think you'd have learned by now — if you're a smart man, you must admit that women are always in charge."

* * *

TWO DAYS LATER, Leo nodded his thanks to the woman who showed him into the back room of the establishment. He chuckled to himself as he pictured his father walking in

159

through the doors, wondering what he would think. He knew Lord Sheriden would have far preferred to meet somewhere like White's if it was to be out of his own home, but Leo needed a location where the staff would keep his presence a secret and where he could actually be afforded a modicum of privacy.

The Red Lion fit all of his requirements. Usually, his visits here were for another purpose, and he hadn't missed the few shameless smiles that some of the serving ladies sent his way, but he found himself entirely unstirred, and he wondered if Georgie had forever ruined him for other women.

He sighed, his ruminations interrupted when his father walked into the room, looking positively disgruntled.

"Father," Leo greeted him as he stood, and his father shook his hand as though they were two strangers meeting for the first time. But that was how his father was. Although all stiff and reserved, Leo knew, deep inside, his father loved his children and would do anything for them. "Thank you for meeting me here."

"I must say I was rather surprised when I received your message."

"I understand. However, I needed somewhere we could speak freely."

His father raised a generous eyebrow but didn't say anything further.

"It has to do with the bill that I encouraged you to put forward last year."

"Yes, that has caused quite the stir in Parliament," his father said, scratching his temple. "I would say the House is evenly divided on the issue. Some believe that our suggestions for increased penalties is too harsh, while others are in complete agreement."

"It likely depends on their own circumstances."

"Such as whether or not they have fought in a duel?" his

father asked wryly. "I must admit that I have not overly pushed it since your disappearance. I didn't have the heart."

"That is a good thing," Leo said and then took a breath, "for I think we need to reconsider the matter."

"You do?" His father raised an eyebrow.

"I do." Leo nodded, remembering the visit to Bedlam to see Georgie's mother. "I still believe that there are people — such as men like Lovelace — who need to be dealt with more severely. However, there are others who are already feeling the brunt of the law upon them."

"What do you propose?" Lord Sheriden asked, crossing his arms and sitting back in his chair as he studied Leo with interest.

"The bill needs rewriting."

"To more severely punish peers?"

"To force them to account for their actions."

The door opened, and they were both silent as they accepted the glasses of brandy offered them.

"The House of Lords will never agree to it, son."

"I know. But we should still try."

"You could be trapping yourself. A duel is illegal and one of the few crimes a man can be punished for rather severely."

"I am aware. But am I not a hypocrite otherwise?"

His father stared at him, the silence disconcerting.

"Tell me, Leopold, what has caused such a change of heart?"

Leo swirled the glass in circles over the scarred mahogany table.

"I have seen the other side of things," he said lowly, "the people who have nothing, who cannot speak for themselves. They are often dealt with far too harshly. The way our current proposed reform is written would cause them further damage than those who are currently not brought to justice at all. We need to separate them out and find the fairest course of action."

"Very well, son," his father said. "Why don't you draw up what you are thinking and then send them to me to look over? In the meantime, I shall announce in Parliament that we are rescinding this bill and will put forward a new one."

"Thank you, Father," Leo said, grateful that his father had always been most reasonable. "How else does the family fare?"

"Well enough," his father said, "we look forward to your return, although we understand the necessity for your own space at this point in time. As it happens, I am on the hunt for a property for you."

"For me?" Leo asked quizzically.

"Of course," his father said with a nod. "I am sure you and your new bride will desire space of your own."

His new bride. Ah, yes. Anne.

"Have you happened to see Anne lately?" Leo asked, hoping that they were nearing the end of this fake betrothal.

"Of course," his father said. "She and her mother are meeting with yours nearly daily. I feel for you, son. While you must be most relieved to avoid all of the planning, you have also quite the event to look forward to."

Dread began to creep down Leo's spine. What was Anne doing? This was supposed to be a temporary measure. Planning a wedding for all the *ton* to gush over was not part of their plans. He needed to talk to her — and quickly.

"I see," he said noncommittedly. "Well, then. Let's get all of this business dealt with so that we can concentrate on the wedding."

"Very good, son," his father said with a nod. "Very good."

CHAPTER 20

"*I*'ll be there in a minute!"

Georgie and Alice exchanged a bemused glance as Alice shrugged. An aged butler didn't bat an eye as he led them into a front parlor, even as there was a loud clunk from the back of the house.

"Never mind Freddie," said Alice's sister-in-law Celeste, who had accompanied them to her friend's house. "She's always working on something or the other."

"What does she do?" Georgie asked curiously, reminding herself to walk slowly, gracefully, as any lady would. She was not used to wearing this fancy of dress but had decided it was warranted when visiting the house of a lady of the *ton*.

"She's an inventor," Alice said with a twinkle in her eye, and Georgie murmured, "I see," even though she was somewhat confused. "Just what does she invent?"

"Oh, a little bit of everything," said, Mrs. Celeste Cunningham, who was married to Alice's brother, Mr. Oliver Cunningham.

Georgie didn't know what exactly she had been expecting, but it was certainly not the small, petite woman with dark brown curls piled high on her head. She walked into the room wiping her hands on a rag, although she greeted them all with a wide smile.

"So lovely to see you all. My apologies. A few things got out of hand back there but all is well now."

After introductions were made, she sat down in a chair, leaning back as she was apparently waiting for one of them to say something.

Georgie finally jumped, realizing that it was her job to do so, even though she was the least ranking woman in the room.

"Thank you for seeing us," she said with a nod. "This may sound odd, but I am one of the Bow Street detectives—"

Lady Dorrington and Mrs. Cunningham exchanged a bit of a chuckle, and Georgie realized that these were women who might not actually find her choice of profession — or any profession — odd at all.

"—And I find myself in a bit of a predicament. You see, the man that I would like to investigate is a marquess and it is difficult for me to discover anything about him."

"I can understand such a predicament," Lady Dorrington murmured. "You are hoping that I can help you, is that it?"

Georgie glanced toward Alice, who confirmed with a nod.

"Yes, I was hoping so. I don't need much — just some information on him, if there are any scandals attached to him or anything that ties him to… the gentleman I am helping."

Freddie's brown gaze focused in on her and Georgie knew she was curious to ask more, but she kept herself from doing so.

"Very well, then," she said with a quick nod. "Who is it?"

Georgie hadn't realized she was going to approach this so quickly, with all of them in the room, but she would take whatever Lady Dorrington offered.

"Lord Marbury."

Lady Dorrington's lips came together as though she had just tasted a sour lemon. "I see."

"What can you tell me about him?"

"Lord Marbury." Lady Dorrington took a breath. "Well, let me see. He is about twenty years my elder, although he always liked to dance with the young ladies at the time I made my coming out, if you know what I mean."

"Is he married?"

"Widowed. Until recently, he has not looked to marry again, or I'm sure some desperate mama would have foisted her poor daughter on him by now."

Georgie focused on her first words.

"What do you mean by 'until recently'?"

"He's suddenly in the market for a wife, which is somewhat surprising considering his age and the fact that he already has the requisite heir and a spare. The only reason I can see for a man his age suddenly desperate for a wife again is that he is in need of her dowry. And from the women in whom he has suddenly become interested, it would appear that the rumors are correct."

"He has suddenly lost it all?" Georgie asked, resting her elbows on her knees as she peered at Lady Dorrington with interest.

She shrugged one of her slim shoulders.

"Apparently. For most noblemen, it is due to heavy losses at the gambling tables or Tattersall's. My husband isn't much for either of those, so I cannot be sure, and I haven't heard much of the gossip."

Perhaps Lord Marbury owed Leo a good sum of money. But why would Leo keep that from her? It seemed innocent enough — unless Leo had done something dubious to be owed such.

"One more thing," Lady Dorrington said, holding up a

finger, "Lord Marbury keeps company with some... less than favorable figures."

"Such as Lord Lovelace?" Georgie asked, crooking up an eyebrow, and Lady Dorrington's pleasant features darkened.

"The very one."

"I'm aware. And I know it doesn't bode well in his favor."

"Just be careful with men like them," Lady Dorrington said with a curt nod.

"Thank you, Lady Dorrington," Georgie said. "This has all been quite helpful."

"Oh, do call me Freddie, everyone does!" the marchioness exclaimed, her friendly countenance returning. "And I apologize that I cannot provide anything else."

"This was wonderful," Georgie said. "It is lovely to meet you."

"Likewise," Freddie beamed. "I cannot say I have ever met a detective, let alone one who is a woman."

"I'm the only one that I know of in London, so that would make sense," Georgie said with a laugh.

The women spent an hour in one another's company before they rose to leave, but Freddie stopped Alice on the way out.

"Will I be seeing you at the wedding?"

"Which wedding?"

Freddie rolled her eyes dramatically. "The Fitzgerald-Belmont wedding. There *is* no other wedding, if you ask the mothers who are involved." She laughed, completely unaware of what the revelation did to Georgie's insides.

She knew Leo had told her that the wedding wasn't anything of consequence, that it was all a farce... but then why would there be such elaborate wedding plans? Did she believe him when he told her there wasn't to actually be a wedding, or was it all part of some elaborate scheme to get her into bed? What did she really know of him? He had ended up leaving because he couldn't bear to be bested by a woman. What did that truly say about him?

It didn't matter, she told herself.

Even though she knew, deep within her, that she was telling herself a lie.

* * *

"Georgie, can I speak to you?"

"Of course."

Marshall sat down beside her earnestly.

"You know the bill, the one about criminal reform that we have been hearing about?"

She sat up straighter. She had been neglectful about her purpose to halt this bill as of late, but that didn't mean that she had completely forgotten about it.

"What about it?"

"There was talk of it today in Parliament."

"There was?"

He nodded slowly. "So I am told. It is, apparently, requiring a rewrite before it actually comes forward."

"Do you know anything about it?" she asked, but he shook his head.

"It's all kept rather secretive for now. I'll do my best to determine what it includes, but I can't imagine that it could be anything good."

"Do you know who is bringing it forward?"

Marshall crossed his arms now, leaning back as he assessed her.

"Now, I don't want you getting upset or anything about this, Georgie. Remember, I'm just giving you the message."

"I am aware," she said dryly. "Don't give me any of that. Continue."

He sighed.

"Very well. The lord who brought it forward is Lord Sheriden."

"Lord Sheriden?" she repeated, her eyebrows rising. "But that is—"

"The Earl of Sheriden, father of your Lord Richmond? Yes. Exactly."

Georgie's stomach dropped as she slammed back against her chair, the wooden nail covers biting into her back. "He's not."

Marshall nodded, then looked away from her as a pained expression covered his face. "Now, I don't know the truth of this, but I'm told… that his son is the one pushing for this."

Georgie went still but for slight tremors that began coursing through her, that she tried to will away but seemed to have a life of their own.

"After everything I told him…" she said, shaking her head with gritted teeth. "That bastard."

"Well, hey now," Marshall said, holding up a hand, "we don't know for certain what the bill includes or what Lord Richmond has to do with it."

"No, we don't," she agreed, "but once Le—Lord Richmond's memories came back, he would have known. He must have."

"Is the Prince losing some of his polish?"

Georgie shot him a nasty look.

"If you're through with harassing me about my friendship with him, I would most truly appreciate it, as it would mean I could get on with my work."

"I'm sorry, Georgie," Marshall said, his face falling as he looked at her with a contrite expression. "You're right, it's not my place. I just don't want to see you hurt, is all."

"Which I appreciate," she said. "But I'm a grown woman who has already been through much in my life. Deception from a lord will not break me."

"But will it break your heart?"

"Absolutely not," she said decisively, sitting up straight. "In fact, I am going to pursue one more avenue of this case, and then after that, I will be done with it. And with him."

"Are you going to speak with Marbury?"

"I am."

"I'll come with you."

"Marshall, I—"

"Georgie, have we ever allowed one another to go after a subject alone in such a situation?"

She sighed. He had her there. "Not usually."

"Exactly. I have to finish this up, and then we'll go."

LEO HAD ALWAYS ENJOYED his life and the freedoms it had offered him.

Which was why he was sick and tired of being prevented from living it out. If Marbury and Lovelace thought that they could frighten him with their threats of death, then it was time they realized that he was not a man to be trifled with, that he could give just as good as he got.

Which was why he now found himself being shown into Lord Marbury's study.

He knew some would take him to be a fool, walking into the lion's den and offering himself up for sacrifice. But as much as he knew that Lovelace had initiated the attacks on him, he was just as aware that both Lovelace and Marbury were too faint of heart to ever pursue such an action. They had others do the work for them.

But Leopold Belmont was not a man who had ever run away with his tail between his legs, and it was time these men realized just who they were dealing with.

"Ah, Marbury, Lovelace. Wasn't sure you would both have the balls to show up."

"Excuse me?" Lovelace stood up indignantly, and Leo rolled his eyes.

"I think we are well past feigned politeness. We passed that when you shot me in the chest, then arranged for me to disappear. Luckily for you, I'm too much of a stubborn ass to allow your attempts to do me in. And then there was the attack in the gardens, Lovelace, when you recognized me. It's unfortunate that a woman was able to best you."

Marbury, the elder of the two, looked to Lovelace with incredulity, and Leo smiled at the well-placed blow.

"I was not bested—" Lovelace began to sputter, but Leo waved a hand in front of his face.

"Not to worry. So were your men in Cheapside just the other day."

"This is all rather barbaric," Marbury said. "Why do we not sit down, have a glass of brandy—"

"I think not. This is not a social call," Leo said with a snort. Besides, he'd rather not chance the brandy. "You will both cease this ridiculous threat against me. If you think that doing away with me will keep you from being charged with attempted murder, you are sorely mistaken."

"You would be charged for dueling just as we would," Marbury countered, but Leo held up a hand.

"I never shot at either of you, so I believe it would be much different."

"I've also heard talk that your father is proposing to put forward a bill that would put us all in jeopardy. How foolish can the two of you be?"

"If a man assaults a woman and then nearly kills her brother multiple times, he should be held accountable."

"We are members of the *nobility*," Lovelace seethed. "We are protected."

"Perhaps," Leo shrugged. "But you have gone to great lengths for a man who is so sure of his own safety."

"You can prove nothing!" Lovelace said, placing a finger in Leo's face. "Nothing at all. In fact, I suggest you take your bill, and shove it up your—"

"Lord Marbury?" they all turned in surprise to find the butler at the door, his dour announcement cutting through the anger in the room. "I apologize, my lord, I tried to stop them, but they refused to wait. I have two Bow Street detectives here to see you."

He stepped out of the way to reveal Marshall and Georgie, who stood there staring with a look of horror upon her face.

CHAPTER 21

*L*eo tried to remember what had been said, tried to determine what Georgie had possibly heard, but from her expression, he knew that it didn't matter.

Whatever she had walked into had been enough. He stared at her in supplication, hoping she would understand, but instead she walked by him and into the room, Marshall following in her wake.

"You called in your woman for protection, did you, Belmont?" Marbury asked, his eyes crinkling into a smile, as Leo realized that any real threat these lords might have felt had vanished when Georgie had arrived.

"I was not aware that Lord Richmond would be here," Georgie said, her voice, as loud and clear as it was, resounding through the dark room that was otherwise devoid of brightness. "Lord Marbury, you were described by Lord Richmond's attackers, so my colleague and I have come to question you."

Lord Marbury looked at her for a moment before throwing back his head and laughing.

"Question me?" he asked. "Whatever for?"

"To ascertain what you have against Lord Richmond that would lead you to hire men to attack him," she said. "Although I believe we already have our answer."

She walked into the room, ignoring the stares of all trained on her, as clearly not one of them there wanted her presence. Marshall remained in the doorframe, arms crossed over his chest as he surveyed them while allowing Georgie to run the room. Leo, however, could feel the man's eyes dance over him with ire.

"We have done nothing wrong," Lord Marbury said, addressing Marshall at the door instead of Georgie. "And you cannot prove we have. In fact, if anything, I would appreciate you escorting this man out of my home. He has come here and done nothing but threaten me and my colleague. I am now fearful for my life."

"Careful, Marbury," Leo drawled, "it sounds as though you just might be asking a woman for help here."

Marbury drew himself up as tall as he could, although the top of his head still only met Leo's chin.

"I am speaking to the Runner at the door."

Georgie and Marshall exchanged a look, and while Leo was perfectly aware that Marshall was but her friend, he longed to be the one who Georgie conversed with unspoken, who was her partner in all aspects.

But he had a feeling that possibility would never be available to him again.

Not with the way Georgie was looking at him, her eyes not just accusatory but... bleak. Sad. Disappointed.

In him.

"I don't believe that Lord Richmond poses a threat to you," Georgie finally said, and Leo held up a hand.

"Not to worry. I will leave of my own will. This company leaves a bad taste in my mouth. Farewell, gentlemen. I encourage you to think on what I've said. For if you continue

173

along this path you have started on, let me assure you that if you take the wrong fork in the road, you could end up somewhere you might later regret."

"You see?" Lovelace huffed. "He is—"

"Good day," Georgie said, tipping her cap, and when she parted the room like a queen and exited, he and Marshall could only fall in behind her.

* * *

"GEORGIE, WAIT."

Leo was not thrilled that he was chasing her down the street like a young pup in love, but nor could he just let her go without at least attempting an explanation.

"I have nothing to say to you," she said when he caught up. He looked to Marshall imploringly, asking for help, but the red-headed man just shook his head in response. "In fact," she continued, her steps even quicker than usual as she seemed to be running away from him, "I do not believe this is a matter for Bow Street any longer. We have fulfilled all that we promised. You know your identity, you have found your rightful place, and you are now aware who it was that attacked you. Unfortunately, we do not have sufficient evidence to convict these gentlemen, and even if we did, we all know that they would receive a pardon simply because of who they are. Noble."

"But that's just the thing," he said earnestly, attempting to keep up, "that is not what I am proposing any longer. I—"

Georgie finally stopped, turning around and slashing her arm between them. "I don't want to hear it. I'm done. With this. With you. I told you everything about me. I took you to meet my *mother*. To meet the *children* that mean everything to me, where I had to live after I was left alone. And all you did was lie to me. This whole time, you were the one who was planning to make things worse for the people that I am fighting for. You were my enemy, the entire time, and you hid it from me."

Marshall stepped away, providing them space, even as passersby sent curious stares their way.

"To be fair, Georgie, I didn't know, not at first. Not when I met your mother or accompanied you—"

"You're right," she said softly. "That is, if you are being honest. It's hard to know what to believe. Did you even lose your memory?"

"I thought you knew when everyone was lying."

She did. And yes, she had been well aware of his sincerity. But at the moment, she was throwing everything she had back at him, questioning both him and herself.

"Besides, what reason would I have for pretending?" Leo asked with exasperation. "For allowing my entire family to think that I was dead? For forcing Perry to believe that he might have to marry the woman I was supposed to?"

"Oh, yes, speaking of that, how is Lady Anne?" Georgie asked, her chin jutted out determinately. "I hear your mother and hers are meeting daily about your wedding."

"Georgie, you know the truth."

"I don't know anything anymore. From what I hear, wedding plans are coming right along quite swimmingly."

Her voice was strong, conviction in each word, and yet he could see the despair in her eyes, the way they flicked back and forth over his face, as though she was but a moment away from breaking.

"Georgie," he said as he stepped closer, lowering his voice so that only she could hear, for this was not a sentiment for anyone but her. "I love you."

She scoffed, looking away from him, her hands on her hips.

"No, you don't."

He stepped back. "Of course I d—"

"You don't. You don't treat someone you love like this. Did you think I would never find out? That I am not competent enough to discover the truth?"

"Georgie, I am changing things. I never realized how this affected people, didn't think—"

"That's just it. You didn't think."

"You have to understand."

"I can't. Not right now. Not today. Leave me alone, Leo."

"But Georgie—"

"We came together under circumstances we never could have imagined. But everything has changed now. Let's be honest, there was never any future for us anyway. For I have no wish to be the wife of a nobleman, and you most certainly could never bring a woman like me into your world. We always knew whatever was between us could only be temporary. Well, that temporary is over now. Thank you for teaching me not to let my guard down, that I must be careful who I trust. I told everyone that they were wrong to warn me against you, but unfortunately, they were right. I was the one who couldn't see the truth."

"Georgie—"

"Goodbye, Leo."

She turned around quickly, just before the tears shimmering in her eyes were about to fall, he was sure of it. Marshall pushed off from where he had been leaning against the building in wait. He looked back, eyeing Leo with warning — a warning not to continue or to come close again.

Leo could do nothing but watch them go.

* * *

"ARE YOU ALL RIGHT?" Marshall hovered in her doorway, obviously worried about leaving her.

"I'm perfectly fine," Georgie said, hoping that her expression didn't betray her. "You have nothing to worry about."

"Georgie," he said softly, tilting his head down to look at her, "you don't have to be the strong one all of the time."

"Yes, I do."

"That's not true."

"Yes, I *do*," she repeated, more emphatically. "You don't understand what it's like to be a woman working in such a profession. To be treated with even an ounce of the respect that you receive, I have to prove that I am not the emotional woman that everyone expects me to be. I can't just be as good as a man. I have to be better. I cannot be ruled by my emotions, which is what I have allowed to happen. From the very moment he asked me not to take him to a hospital, when he required additional protection, I allowed my emotions to rule me. I should have said no."

Marshall, usually not one to look particularly deep into such matters, sighed as he stared at her for a moment before speaking, as though wondering whether or not he should say anything.

"Georgie, here's the thing," he said, stepping into the room and closing the door behind him. "Any man or woman can make decisions based on fact alone. However, it is not your feelings but your *intuition* that makes you good at what you do, that sets you apart from others. It is nothing to be ashamed of."

"I didn't think so either," she said bitterly, "until now."

"Why don't you come for dinner tonight?" he asked, raising an eyebrow, but she shook her head. She was not fit for company.

"I told Abby that I would come Sunday. I'll wait until then. The last thing she needs is another night with another mouth to feed."

Marshall eyed her. "You know she doesn't mind."

"I know. But still. If it's all the same, I would like to be alone."

"Very well. But if you need anything—"

"I know where to find you. Thank you, Marshall."

When he finally acceded to her wishes and shut the door behind him, Georgie sank down into one of the chairs, too stunned to allow any emotions to surface. She was just tired. Tired of trying. Tired of feeling things that she had no right to feel. For the truth was, she did love Leo. Except the Leo she loved was the man she had fished out of the Thames, not the man she had come to know once he had regained his memories. And that was who he was. He wasn't going to change or revert back to the man she had first met.

That was a fact she had to accept, and she hated it as much as she loved him.

Finally, from deep within her, the turmoil that had been swirling in her gut began to rise, until it bubbled over the surface and spilled out in a sob that nearly choked her.

She leaned down over the table, her fingers hitting smooth metal as she did so. Leo's medallion. She wrapped her hand around the metal and hugged it tightly to her chest as she placed her forehead on her arms, and allowed it all to flow out.

* * *

"What's the matter with you?"

"Nothing."

Sarah eyed him with chagrin. "I know that is not true."

"Drop it, Sarah," Leo muttered. "It doesn't matter."

He had arrived at his family's home just in time for wedding planning. He had tried to shove off the invitation, until he had found out that Lady Anne would be there. It was about time that they had a discussion about what was happening with this blasted wedding.

"You've never been a particularly affable sort, but you have been downright surly ever since you arrived," Sarah said, her nose in the air. "You didn't say a word through tea, and have simply grunted every time someone says anything to you."

"Aren't you busy with your own wedding plans?"

She sniffed. "I have been waiting a long time for the wedding of my dreams. I will not allow your hastily arranged affair to get in the way nor provide a distraction. With Basil away at the moment, we shall wait until the timing is perfect for our own nuptials."

"I still can't believe that the two of you got together."

She shrugged. "Sometimes you find love where you least expect it."

Wasn't that the truth.

She tilted her head as she eyed him critically. "You haven't been the same since you returned."

"Coming close to death can change a man."

"True," she said with a nod. "But there's more to it. You're... softer."

"I am not soft," he said, enunciating each word with power to show how much he meant them as he stood and walked over to the sideboard, pouring himself a brandy.

"Perhaps softer is the wrong word," she decided. "Kinder."

"You must be thinking of your other brother."

"Fine," she said with a dramatic sigh. "Don't talk to me about it then. But for goodness sake, you better erase that frown from your face before Lady Anne walks in and decides that she no longer has any desire to marry a sourpuss like you."

That was the goal, actually.

"Ah, here she is now," Sarah said brightly, standing and greeting Anne and her mother as they walked into the room.

Before the ladies could begin on their frivolous plans, Leo, having no time nor inclination to partake in any of it, interrupted right at the beginning.

"Lady Anne, may I speak to you alone for a moment?" he asked, as four pairs of shocked eyes swung toward him.

"Leopold, I don't think—" his mother began, but he quelled her protest with a dark look that had her snapping her mouth shut. "Very well. Go into the parlor but keep the door open."

"Obviously."

As the women gaped at him, he held out his elbow to Anne, knowing that he was going to hear an earful from his mother once their company had left them.

"Anne," he said when they finally had a moment alone, "what is going on?"

"Oh, Leo," she said with a sigh, rubbing her hands together nervously from her perch on the edge of the sofa, her voice low as she looked at him, "I'm so sorry. I had wanted to explain all to you, but wasn't sure how to contact you."

"I'm here now," he said, crossing his arms over his chest as she stood, seemingly unable to sit still, leaving him and walking to look out the window. "Explain away."

He studied her profile, unable to help himself from comparing her to Georgie. Anne was what every English gentleman was supposed to want in a wife. A fragile beauty, courteous and biddable and from the proper family.

But she was not what he wanted. Not any longer. He couldn't help himself. He wanted a woman who was tall, strong, dark-haired and sharp-tongued, who said what she pleased, when she pleased, whose mother currently resided in Bedlam, even though she was no more insane than his own mother.

"I tried to tell my mother about Clark, but she was so aghast she made me promise not even to mention him to Father. But not to worry — Clark and I have a plan."

"Oh?" He raised a brow.

"It does involve you, I am afraid." Despite the trepidation underlying her tone, her eyes were bright with glee as she turned to him now, her hands still together, but in excited happiness. "I will accompany my father to the church. When we arrive, you will be standing there at the front and I would ask that Clark be one of the men standing up with you. Then at the last moment, you simply switch places."

"Anne..." Leo began, shaking his head before she even finished. "That is a disastrous plan. Why don't you just run away or something, like everyone else does when their parents don't approve?"

Her face fell. "Oh, Leo, I know it's a lot to ask of you, but I really would like to be married with my family there. Even if they don't agree to it. My sister would be so disappointed if she didn't see me married, and my little nieces... please, Leo, will you do it?"

He rubbed a hand over his face. "What of the marriage contract?"

"We would have to speak with the minister beforehand and obtain a common license as the banns will not have been read. Perhaps if you accompanied Clark to the Doctor's Commons? The Archbishop would do it if you asked it of him, Leo, I know he would."

"Your name would be forever mired in scandal. So would mine."

She sent her gaze to the floor.

"I understand if it's too much to ask, Leo, truly I do. I'm sorry. I—"

"I, however, don't altogether care what people think of me. My brother is already married and my sister is betrothed to my brother's closest friend, so it is not as though anyone will have cause to shun us. My mother may have an apoplexy and my father may never forgive me, but, at the moment, I have done far worse."

"I'm not sure I understand."

"You don't have to," he said, waving his hand dismissively. "I've done something irrevocable to hurt someone that I love, that is all."

"Oh, Leo," she said, stepping toward him and placing a hand on his arm. "Have you found love?"

"I thought I did," he said gruffly, "but she will never be with me, not now that she knows the truth of what I have done that so hurt her."

"If you love her — and if she loves you — then you can make it work. I know you can," Anne said earnestly. "You are the same man who overcame death, who was too stubborn to lose his memories for the rest of his life. I'm sure you can convince this woman that love is worth it."

"Maybe," he said morosely. "Maybe not."

CHAPTER 22

*G*eorgie would never forgive him.

She promised herself that the next morning as she laced up her boots. Never, since her mother had been taken from her and locked away for the rest of her life, had Georgie's heart ever been so broken.

It was a feeling that she did not appreciate, and she vowed to never allow it to happen to her again.

Now she was sitting across from her mother, wishing she could do more to help her plight.

"I am going to try to intercede for you again," Georgie said, leaning forward on her elbows to look at her. "There has to be something I can do."

"Oh, don't worry overly about me," her mother said, waving a hand. "You should be getting on with your life, finding a man to spend it with, one who will make you happy. What about the one who was here with you last time?"

Georgie snorted as she stood and crossed her arms, pacing the three steps back and forth in the small room.

"He is no one."

"Oh, Georgie, what happened?"

"Nothing." She forced a smile onto her face, even though it felt like it was going to crack her cheeks to do so. "He just wasn't right for me."

"You seemed to get on so well. I had hoped—"

"Don't worry about me, Mother," Georgie said, knowing she had stayed longer than she should have, but unable to tear herself away. "I shall see you soon, all right?"

Her mother nodded, and Georgie wrapped her arms around her in a tight embrace before she followed the attendant through the corridors until she returned to the outside London air that, while not exactly fresh, was at least better than that inside the hospital.

She balled her hands into fists as she stomped through the muck, uncaring that it splashed on her boots and her trousers. She wanted to leave this case behind her, but she had always been a person to see things through. She had one stop to make — two men she must question, before they were no longer available to her.

"Are you sure about this?" Frank, one of her colleagues, asked as he let her into the jail where the two men were being held.

"I am." she nodded, stepping into the cell, where the two men awaited.

"Ah, look who it is."

Hairs on the back of her neck stood up at the voices. She told herself to ignore them, to ask them what she had come here for.

It didn't help.

"The woman saviour. The one who has been keeping Lord Leo out of trouble."

"That's enough," she snapped, waving a hand toward them as though swatting away a fly.

"Oh, are we bothering you?" The one man stepped toward

her. While she slightly recoiled at the smell of him, she was not particularly frightened. They were in the middle of a prison, and, if required, she knew that one of the guards would have enough compassion to come to the rescue of a lone woman against two brutes. That is, if she actually needed it. She had bested them before, and now with this pent up anger raging within her, she highly doubted she would have any troubles again.

"I told you that was *enough*."

"Did Lord Leo get rid of you? Tire of you as a mistress? Can't see how those trousers would turn him on."

Georgie was finished with the man who was tap dancing behind her, calling his barbed words over her shoulder. She whipped around and planted her fist in his face.

He cried out in painful surprise, and she looked up at the second man, hoping he could understand just how ruthless she currently felt.

"Care to take the next shot?"

"No," he said, shaking his head rapidly. He looked around quickly and then leaned in. "You know... I like a woman who can look after herself."

She snorted and stepped back, crossing her arms.

"Are you all right in there?" the guard asked behind her, and she nodded grimly.

"Just fine."

"How about the prisoners?" the man asked with a chuckle.

"Would you bestow your favours on me if I took care of your Lord Leo? Word is there is a job up for hire. You just need to get us out of here in time."

"What are you talking about?" she asked, rounding on him.

His eyes grew in size at the ferocity of her words as he began to back away.

"N-nothing. Only his wedding is soon and I've heard that whoever stops it — stops him — will be well compensated."

"Who has the job?" she demanded, knowing the only way to determine the true perpetrators behind this was to get them through an informant.

"That's the thing," the man said with a shrug. "No one is hired. Whoever does the job gets the money."

"For frig's sake," Georgie said, wiping a hand across her brow.

For the truth was, as much as she despised Leo and all he had done, she loved him in equal measure. She couldn't allow anything to happen to him, nor to his friends or family, many of whom were her own.

She had to go warn him.

* * *

"ROSE, I need to speak with Leo, but I cannot find him anywhere."

"Georgie," Rose stood from her makeshift work table, which was littered in fossils, concern on her face as she greeted her friend. "Is everything all right?"

"No, everything is not all right."

"If this is about the wedding…" Rose looked from one side to the other as though determining that no one was listening, then lowered her voice to speak to Georgie. "I don't believe that Leo or Anne are as committed to it as one might think."

"I know, but then why are they going through with it?" Georgie asked, unable to help the desperation in her tone, hating it and wishing it away.

"I'm not sure what exactly is happening," Rose said, "but there seems to be an awful lot of secrecy surrounding it. As for where you can find Leo, Perry might know and I have a couple of ideas. But first, tell me, what is wrong?"

"I have reason to believe that Leo — and anyone who attends the wedding — will be in danger."

She quickly told Rose the story.

Rose's eyes, the color of the night sky that glinted like the stars, widened as Georgie spoke. "You think someone will kill Leo at the wedding?"

"I do," Georgie said firmly. "But I'm afraid if I say anything, I will just look the desperate fool who doesn't want him to wed."

"Oh, Georgie," Rose said softly, "you love him, don't you?"

"I—" Georgie opened her mouth but then promptly closed it again, as Rose looked at her with pity she had no desire for. "It doesn't matter. I need to talk to him. I don't want to put every person in that church in danger."

"You could try his new living quarters, although I'm not sure whether he will be there," Rose said, providing her the address. "And Georgie, if you ever need to talk more about it, please, just let me know."

"I will," Georgie said softly. "Not to worry."

Leo, however, was not to be found in his new accommodations. Everywhere she looked, Georgie was reminded of him but couldn't actually find him.

She had hoped to never see him again, had no idea how she would ever face him, knowing how much she wanted him yet how much she despaired of that very fact.

She had one final option. She tucked her hair up into her cap and opened the door of what she knew to be his club, The Red Lion. She had learned long ago that the best way to enter a place one was not supposed to be was to simply pretend to belong.

She didn't make it very far.

She had only walked a few steps into the entrance,

187

attempting to keep her head down and not look all over the place in awe like a ninny. It didn't stop an arm from stretching out in front of her.

"Excuse me, sir, but I must ask if you are a member or have an invitation?"

"I'm here to meet a friend," she said in her gruffest voice.

"Who would that be?" the doorkeeper asked.

"Lord Richmond."

"I'm sorry, but Lord Richmond is not—"

"It's fine, Anderson, he's with me."

Georgie looked up in surprise at the deep voice that was both familiar and yet strange to her.

And found herself staring into the sea-green eyes that she knew and loved so well. Only, these didn't belong to Leo. They were surrounded by a few more wrinkles, with a silver mane of hair stretching above them.

"Lord Sheriden," she couldn't help but blurt out, forgetting to lower her voice. The footman stepped toward them, but Lord Sheriden held out a hand. "Anderson, a private room, if you don't mind?"

"Yes, my lord," the footman said, leading them down the hall, although he looked back over his shoulder a few times as though checking to see if his eyes had deceived him or if he had been accurate in his assessment that Georgie was not the man she was pretending to be.

Lord Sheriden said nothing until they were seated around an ornate mahogany table, a hunting scene that Georgie found quite obscene staring down at them from a huge painting on the wall, but then, no one had asked her opinion.

"Miss Jenkins, isn't it?" Lord Sheriden asked, sitting back, crossing one leg over his other.

"Yes, it is," she said with a slight nod in a low voice.

"May I ask what you are doing here, at my son's club?"

"I was trying to find him, my lord," she said, sitting forward in her chair.

"That makes two of us."

"Oh, dear," she said, worried that none of them could find Leo. "You see, I've come across some information. There are men who will attempt to take your son's life at his wedding tomorrow. It must be stopped."

She wasn't sure what she had expected from Lord Sheriden. She had assumed that he would be shocked, or, at the very least, grateful that she had brought such information to him. Instead, he simply sat there, assessing her.

"Miss Jenkins," he said slowly and not unkindly, and yet she could hear the reproach in his voice. "I am aware that you and my son spent a great deal of time together before he regained possession of his memories."

"We did, my lord, but—"

"Now that he is once again Lord Richmond, he has certain... duties that he has to attend to. One of those is marrying Lady Anne."

Georgie was silent for a moment, collecting her thoughts, realizing that Lord Sheriden thought she was trying to stop the wedding because she wanted Leo to herself. She snorted inwardly. If only he knew the full story.

"I understand that, Lord Sheriden, better than you know," she said in a steady, even tone. "However, I am concerned for everyone in attendance at the wedding. Lord Lovelace and Lord Marbury are quite eager to see Lord Richmond's demise."

She couldn't sit still any longer. She stood up and began walking back and forth a few paces one way and then the other along the short end of the top of the table.

"The bill that you are pushing forward at the urging of your son—" She couldn't help the contempt that entered her voice even as she spoke of it. "—it would see lords such as

189

these more likely to be held accountable for their actions. Of course, there is much to say about what else such a bill would do, but for now, this is the concern. They feel that if your son is no longer a threat, that you would not follow up with it."

Lord Sheriden followed her with his eyes before nodding slowly, his stillness more apparent in contrast to Georgie's restlessness.

"I understand, Miss Jenkins. This bill seems to have caused quite the misunderstanding."

"What do you mean?"

He sighed, pushing back his chair and standing, likely so that he was not looking up at her. She guessed that a man such as he far preferred to look down at people — especially people like her.

"My son was most insistent when he returned that we were presenting it all wrong. That by putting forward the bill as we were, there were too many innocent — or near-innocent — people who were going to become caught up in it. We have actually rewritten it." He paused. "Now, the truth is that we have not changed much that would affect lords such as Lovelace and Marbury. But they don't know that. Not yet."

At his initial words, Georgie had stopped pacing, stopping and staring at him.

"Wh-what did you say?"

He looked down his nose at her, and she realized she was being rather rude.

"Pardon me, my lord. Could you please explain further about the bill? What exactly was changed?"

"Nothing is completed yet. It still has to go through the appropriate channels. But Leo was quite insistent that he had not previously fully grasped what his bill would do and that it required amendments. Truthfully, I wasn't sure putting forward the bill at first, but Leo had such enthusiasm for it that I didn't want to discourage him."

Georgie's fingers curled around the back of the chair in front of her as she found she needed something to lean against. She had accused Leo of so much. Perhaps she had been right, at least at first. He was clearly the man she had thought he had been before she had pulled him from the river.

But then she had assumed that he had remained that man once he regained his memories. But she had been wrong. He *had* changed — or, at least, had remembered some of himself as he had been before his memories had returned.

He had certainly learned from what she had shown him, had tried to make a difference. And she had turned him away.

Oh, God... her heart ached desperately. She took a breath as she tried to rein in all of her emotions, which were threatening to rapidly gallop away from her.

"Are you all right, Miss Jenkins?"

"I think so," she managed, looking up to find that Lord Sheriden was staring at her with some concern.

"I appreciate your warning for tomorrow. But I cannot see men like Lovelace or Marbury allowing such a thing to happen on holy ground. All will be fine. Besides," he murmured, "if I put a stop to an event, I will be the one who will breathe my last once my wife gets a hold of me."

"Very well," Georgie said, understanding she wasn't going to get any further with him. "Thank you for your time, Lord Sheriden. And for not turning me away."

"You have done much for my family, Miss Jenkins," Lord Sheriden said with a slight upturn of his lips, and Georgie realized that beneath his strong, regal exterior, he was a man who cared. "I would never turn you away."

She nodded, collecting her cap from where she had left it on the table.

"Good day, Lord Sheriden."

ELLIE ST. CLAIR

"Good day, Miss Jenkins."

As Georgie set foot back onto the steps outside the club after a most belligerent stare down from the footman, who obviously felt that his responsibilities had been compromised, she took a breath. She had been wrong. So wrong. And she knew now that she loved Leo, with all of her heart. He had tried to change things — for her. But now he was getting married, to someone else. She had no idea if he was going to go through with the wedding but she also knew he was too honorable to simply cry off. If Anne hadn't stopped the wedding by now, had she changed her mind? Was she also going to go ahead and do her duty to her family?

It wasn't for Georgie to stop the wedding. If he chose to marry Anne, then so be it. The two of them would be much better together than she and Leo ever would be. They clashed like oil and water. It was fiery, yet the flames could burn to the point where they were absolutely terrifying. But when they exploded... no. She wouldn't think of it.

And all that being said — she could never fit herself into the role of a countess. She was a detective, for goodness' sake.

She would do the only thing that she could. She would make sure that Leo was safe, as were the rest of his family and friends. She could at least do that for him, after he had done so much for her, even if she hadn't known about it.

There was only one thing left to do — even if it killed her, she was going to have to go to the damn wedding.

CHAPTER 23

*L*eo tugged on his cravat. He wore one daily, but today it was so restricting he would have thought it had been tied in order to choke him.

"Craven will be most annoyed if you ruin his perfectly tied cravat."

Leo looked at his brother in the mirror. Perry lounged in a chair on the far side of the room. He had been silently observing Leo, who was pacing the room, adjusting his clothing multiple times, rubbing a thumb over his already shining shoes.

"Leo," Perry said slowly, "Do you *want* to get married?"

"Yes."

Which wasn't a lie. He did want to marry — just not the woman who was going to appear at the church today.

He understood Anne's plan, and he would do what he could to help it along. He just wasn't sure if Anne was the type of woman who would actually go through with it. Not with a church full of people and a family who expected otherwise of her.

If Clark wasn't there, if Anne asked Leo to continue with the wedding, could he do it?

"Leo," Perry stood now, walking behind him and meeting his gaze in the mirror. "What is happening? I thought you and Anne loved each other."

Leo grunted. "We did — to a point. In the past."

"But not anymore?" Perry's eyes widened.

Leo sighed. "It's complicated."

"Well, you don't have much time to figure it out."

Leo studied his brother for a moment. He had so often discounted Perry, not giving him a second thought. Perry spent so much time lost in his dreams, in his paintings, which Leo could never understand, so tied was he to the world around him and all of the responsibilities awaiting him. But he also knew that Perry had been through quite a bit himself, had determined that he was more than what everyone thought he was, had stood up for what he believed in and desired for himself and proved that happiness and duty could coexist.

Leo had always told Perry what to do, had certainly never sought advice from him. And yet, perhaps his younger brother had some wisdom to impart.

"I'll have to make this quick," Leo said. "But here we go."

As succinctly as he could, he told Perry about meeting Georgie, staying with her, meeting her mother, and then regaining his memories and leaving her. He told Perry about the danger he was in, about the bill and what Georgie had thought of his lie of omission. He told him about Anne's plan and his fear of what she would actually do once they arrived at the church.

Perry was silent as Leo explained it all, and Leo was grateful that his brother had always been a good listener.

When Leo finished, Perry was still for a moment, and Leo knew from past experience that his brother was reflecting on the situation before he made any of his own judgements.

"Well," he said slowly, exhaling as he did. "That is quite the conundrum."

"Yes."

"It's also quite simple."

"How so?"

"Do you love her?"

"Who?"

Perry rolled his eyes. "Georgie."

Leo paused for a beat. It was something he had barely admitted to himself, let alone to Perry. "Yes."

"Well, you don't have to sound so excited about it."

Leo rolled his eyes. "I have... taken steps to try to win her back. If I can get through the first part of the plan, then the second can go into action, at least, if all goes well — and if Georgie can ever forgive me. Only, there is one potential downfall."

"Lady Anne."

"Yes, Lady Anne. She has to follow through. The only way to call the wedding off is if she does so herself."

"You have always been an honourable man, Leo. Except to yourself."

"What do you mean?"

"How is that fair to you? Or to Lady Anne herself, for the two of you to live a life together without love?"

"Perry, if I cry off, she will be forever ruined. It would be too scandalous to overcome."

Perry shoved his hands in his pockets, and walked over to the window, looking down.

"How sure did she seem that she was going to go ahead and marry Clark?"

"At the time, quite sure."

Perry turned to him with a small smile. "Well, then, I

suppose you will just have to trust that she will do as she promised. Then you will have to go after Georgie."

"Perry—"

"You love her. From all accounts, she loves you. That is enough to overcome anything."

Leo good-naturedly cuffed his brother on the shoulder, the only way he knew how to show affection.

"You are quite the romantic."

"I know," Perry said with a grin, and then strolled out the door. Leo could only follow.

* * *

GEORGIE HOPED she was out of sight behind the pillar in front of St. George's. She wore her cap low over her eyes, hoping that she wouldn't be recognized. She had worn her breeches, as she had no intentions of actually going into the church — especially not if it meant she would be witnessing Leo marry another woman — unless she absolutely had to. And if that was the case, it would mean that she'd require her breeches in order to move fluidly as she would be going after a murderer.

A parade of carriages continued to go by, some stopping to allow their elegant passengers to disembark and hurry up the stairs to witness what was supposed to be the "wedding of the season" according to the newspapers. Georgie usually did read the gossip pages, if only to see whether there were any shreds of truth in them that could help her with her investigations.

Certainly *not* to see if there was any mention of Leo.

She should have brought Alice with her. For while she recognized some of the people stepping into the church, how was she to know if there was anyone entering who had no business in being there?

A familiar crest appeared on one of the carriages, and Georgie ducked back behind the pillar, glancing around it to see Leo, Perry, Rose, and Lord and Lady Sheriden disembark. Lady Sheriden seemed most pleased, the only one in the group talking as they strode up the steps and into the church. Georgie noted that Lord Sheriden did seem to be somewhat on edge, looking about him as they entered, and she hoped that her warning had gotten through to him.

She was so intent on the family that she yelped when a figure suddenly appeared right beside her.

"Marshall!" she hissed, placing a hand over her rapidly beating heart. "You nearly scared me to death."

"I thought you expected me."

"No! I just told you what was happening to see if you could glean any information."

"Well, I'm just glad that you came to me this time instead of Drake."

"Drake's here too," she muttered.

"What?"

"He's around the other side, keeping watch on the back entrance."

"We better be getting paid well for this," Marshall grumbled, crossing his arms over his chest.

"Actually... we're not."

"Pardon me?"

"The family didn't ask us here. But, Marshall, I can't very well just leave them all here alone like leading lambs to the slaughter."

"Georgie, we have no business being here."

"If you want to leave, you can go and I will not judge you for it. But I have a friend in there, and I will not leave her."

"Or him."

"Who?"

"Richmond."

"Fine, or Lord Richmond. Are you happy now?"

She knew that Marshall shouldn't be the recipient of her anger, but he was bothering her, and she wished he would leave her to suffer her misery alone.

"Very well. I'll go to the other side."

"If you see anything, you know what to do."

"The bird call. Of course I know. How many times have we been in situations like this?"

She nodded and he began to walk away but stopped, looking back at her for a moment, narrowing his eyes as he scrutinized her face.

"Georgie... sometimes it's more difficult to think clearly when your heart is involved. Be careful, all right?"

She nodded. "Always."

Her eyes flicked back and forth, watching, and when a hack pulled to a stop in front of the church, she came alert. No one who was invited to this wedding would be arriving in a hack. They would all have their own carriages.

The man who emerged was, however, well dressed, as much as the groom himself. His fingers nervously pulled at the cuffs of his jacket as he walked up the stairs. Georgie wondered if she should stop him, if this was a man who had dressed for the occasion to try to disguise who he actually was. She had just taken a step out from behind the pillar when she stopped. She recognized him. This was Clark — the man who worked with Madeline and who, apparently, Anne had feelings for. What was *he* doing here? Was he here for punishment? He must be made of stronger stuff than she, for she could never bring herself to voluntarily enter the church.

Only a couple of minutes later, one last carriage pulled up — the Montrose carriage. A man who must be Anne's father alighted, followed by Lady Montrose, and then Anne herself. She was a breathtaking vision, wearing white and carrying a bouquet of cream and pale pink flowers that were as delicate as she was.

She looked at her parents with a small, scared smile, before they led her up the stairs and into the church.

Georgie exhaled, pushing all of the air out. It was nearly done, then. Leo was about to be a married man. And she would never see him again.

In the meantime, she would assure he was alive, and then she would leave, and he would never know she had been here nor what he actually meant to her.

She was distracted from her reveries by another carriage that pulled to a stop. She didn't recognize the crest, but narrowed her eyes when Lord Lovelace stepped out. Of all the— but then instead of driving away, the driver jumped down to the street in his livery, marking him as a servant. Lovelace's servant?

Georgie began mounting the stairs, stopping beneath the majestic portico. She leaned against one of the Corinthian columns just as Lovelace approached.

"Excuse me," he said with a wide, sickly sweet smile. Georgie lifted a brow.

"You are not going in there."

"That is for you to say?" he asked, his nostrils flaring.

"I am well aware that you are not invited, my lord, and I'm not sure why you would have any reason to enter these church doors."

He scoffed. "Come now, you truly don't think I would try anything in a church, do you?"

Georgie stood tall and crossed her arms over her chest.

"I think the family would prefer that you leave."

"And just what would you know about what the family would want, hmm?" He stepped closer to her, and Georgie hated the fact that he was taller than she, allowing him to look down on her. "Maybe when your viscount didn't know who he was, it was all well and good for you to play the Cinderella story with him. But he's a lord, Miss Runner, and he is going to marry his Lady Anne. I am a friend of her mother's cousin, Lord Marbury. Now, step aside and allow me to join the festivities."

Georgie was about to tell him just exactly what he could do with his command, when she heard the bang of the door, and she whirled around to see the church door closing, the driver gone.

Marshall was already running from the other side, and Georgie wasted no more than half a second on the smirking Lord Lovelace before she rushed in after him.

The servant was advancing down the side of the church, closing in as he passed pew after pew. Georgie refused to take her eyes off him as she chased him down, even though in her periphery she could see the pair standing at the front before the vicar. She dimly noted the murmurings humming through the church, and she wondered whether everyone realized what was happening. Had they noted the driver and questioned his presence? Surely not. How would they have any idea—

Her thoughts were cut off when she saw the servant stop and pull a pistol out of his pocket. Georgie didn't have any time to get a hold of her own weapon. She sprinted the last few strides and launched herself from her feet, connecting with the driver — if that was even what he was — in a flying leap. The pistol he had been aiming went off erratically into the air, and the crowd that filled the pews seemed to let out a collective shriek. Georgie prayed that no one had been hit as she and the assailant wrestled on the ground in their battle to grasp hold of the weapon.

The man was quicker than she was, just managing to recapture his hold on it. He was stronger too, and struggle as Georgie might, she found herself beneath him, as he sat on her chest and pointed the barrel of the gun right between her eyes.

"You are a nuisance, you know that?" he grunted.

Georgie tried to fight him off, twisting and squirming, doing everything she could to force his grasp to release, but with sinking horror she realized she didn't have enough time nor enough strength. She squeezed her eyes, bracing for the impact, but it didn't come — instead of hearing the shot, she heard the sickening sound of flesh meeting flesh followed by a grunt, and the weight loosened off her chest.

When she opened her eyes, it wasn't the attacker that filled her visage, but a very familiar face — one that she saw every night when she closed her eyes.

"It's about time I was the one to save you," Leo said with a grin, and if Georgie was a swooner, now would have been the time to do so.

She, however, was nothing of the sort, and she forced herself to her feet, looking around to see first that Leo had knocked out her attacker, and second, that the entire church was now nearly empty, most people having likely run off after the gunshot. Even their curiosity was overcome by the need to protect themselves.

But how were there two people still standing in front of the vicar? One was Anne, yes, who had fainted — swooned, Georgie supposed, she definitely struck her as a swooner — but the man who held her was not Leo. She looked back and forth from Leo to the altar, confusion reigning when she saw Clark was standing up with Lady Anne.

"What in the hell is happening here?" she said incredulously, earning a frown from the vicar.

"Excuse me, Father," she said, but then turned her head back to Leo. "Leo?"

He stepped toward her, dipping his head close to her ear.

"Anne is marrying Clark. She has wanted to from the

beginning," he murmured, even as Georgie looked side to side to see his parents looking on with concern but not complete anger. "Which is the perfect ending, as there is another I wish to marry."

He shocked her by kneeling down in front of her.

"Georgina Jenkins, will you be my wife?"

Georgie's mouth gaped open. Was this all some sick joke? For he couldn't be asking her this — here — *now* — could he?

"I—I—" she stammered. "I d-d—"

She stopped as a figure over Leo's shoulder prevented all thought. "Mother?"

Georgie must have been shot and was now in some insane purgatory. That was the only rational answer for this handsome lord at her feet and her mother standing in a new dress at the end of a pew in St. George's Church.

"Well?" her mother prodded, waving her hands toward her. "Answer the poor man!"

"I called in a few favors," Leo said huskily, looking up at Georgie, "and I promise to do all I can to right the wrongs so that others don't end up in her situation."

"Thank you," she whispered, tears brimming in her eyes.

"There's something else you should know."

She didn't know if she could take anymore.

"Yes?"

"After Anne and Clark finish up, the vicar is free to do one more ceremony. I have a special license. I thought I'd have to come find you after this, but since you have conveniently shown up... I love you. And I want to marry you. So I suppose the question is — will you marry me... today?"

CHAPTER 24

Georgie looked down at herself. She was wearing breeches and a shirt and jacket, which were not only dishevelled, but torn.

She knew most women would be asking for words of love, for a fancy speech with frivolous words of all that Leo felt for her. But she wasn't that woman. She didn't need him to tell her what he felt. He had shown her already with his actions, for all that he had done for her.

She was enough for him. And that worked just fine for her. "You know I can't dance."

"I know."

"You know that I'm not much for attending all those fancy balls and parties."

"I know."

"You know I won't give up my breeches."

"I hope you never do."

"And I will always want to work… in some way."

"I can't imagine you not doing so."

"Yes," she said, blinking back tears that threatened. She cleared the lump that had formed in her throat. "Yes, I will."

He opened his mouth as a crease formed between his eyes, but then he stopped — and she realized he had likely thought she was going to say no.

"Did you just say yes?" His eyes opened wider in astonishment.

"Didn't you hear me?"

She tugged on his hands, urging him to rise to his feet so that he was standing in front of her, so they could look one another in the eyes.

"If we do this, though, Leo," she said intently, "there is no going back. Are you sure?"

His eyes bore into hers with an equal intensity. "I've never been surer of anything in my life."

She believed him. He was not a man who did anything in half measures.

He reached up to her neck, trailing his fingers along the chain peeking out from beneath her shirt.

"You're wearing my medallion."

She grinned up at him.

More murmuring began at the front of the church, and Georgie turned to see that Anne had come to her feet with a smile and a wave to all. When the vicar asked her if she would like to continue, she nodded, even as her mother called out that perhaps they should wait for another time — a time that she likely wished to prevent from ever occurring.

"No, no, Mother," she said, even as the curious gossips began to filter in from the back of the church, unable to keep themselves away from the drama that was apparently occurring within. It worked to Anne's favor, as it meant that her parents would keep themselves from creating any additional scandal.

"Very well." Her mother sighed as she fanned her flushed face, likely near to swooning herself. "Go ahead."

And so as Marshall and Drake dealt with Lord Lovelace and his hired help, Georgie and Leo took a seat, with Georgie's mother on the other side of her, as they watched Anne marry the man who was the true love of her life. Georgie had to pinch herself a couple of times just to ensure that this was all actually occurring. Leo frowned at her in query, but she just smiled and shook her head, unable to explain until afterward.

When Anne and Clark were announced husband and wife and then linked arms and began to walk out of the church with smiles as wide as Georgie could ever imagine, Leo held out his hand to her, and asked, "Ready?"

Georgie's mother nodded at her encouragingly, but it wasn't her mother's opinion she was most concerned about. While it wouldn't have entirely held her back, she hoped that Leo's parents would accept her. It would be a long, lonely life without the support of his family.

"Leo," she murmured in his ear before they approached the altar. "Perhaps we best speak to your parents first."

"No, it's fine," he said, shaking his head with a determined glint in his eyes.

She refused to step forward, tugging on his hand with insistence. Realizing she would not be deterred, he sighed and turned around to his parents, who were sitting in the front pew wearing matching looks of concern.

"Mother, Father," he said in a low, deep tone so that they were the only ones who would hear his address. "I must apologize for the deception. Lady Anne was in a difficult place and requested my help. I couldn't say no to her."

"You have embarrassed us," his mother hissed.

"For that, I am most sorry," he said, tilting his head as he noted her concern. "But it has allowed me the chance to marry the woman with whom I have fallen in love. Georgina Jenkins."

"I understand this isn't the most idyllic time or setting," Georgie noted. "And I am happy to wait—"

"No," Leo said resolutely, his gaze burning into her. "We will be married today."

"The woman is wearing breeches!" his mother said incredulously, but all were surprised when Lord Sheriden placed a hand over his wife's.

"If this is the woman who will keep Leo happy, then this is his choice," he said in a low tone. "We allowed Perry to marry the woman he loved. Why should we expect any different for Leo?"

"Because he is the heir," Lady Sheriden insisted.

"We thought Perry would be as well at his wedding."

"But Perry *needed* Rose to fulfill his duties."

"And I need Georgie," Leo said somberly. "Perhaps I would have been fine had I not met her, but now that I know and love her as I do, I cannot live a life without her."

His parents exchanged a look that must have said more than words ever could, for finally his mother nodded, albeit with some hesitation.

"Very well, Leo, marry whom you want."

She looked to her husband. "You are aware we shall now forever be known as the family of scandal."

Her husband snorted. "Let them say what they want. At least our children will be happy. Isn't that what is most important in life?"

While Georgie would never swoon, Lord Sheriden's words nearly knocked her right over. She certainly would never have imagined them coming from a peer, let alone Leo's father.

"Very well," Leo said, turning to Georgie. "*Now* can we be married?"

"In breeches?" she asked, her lips curling upward.

"I wouldn't have it any other way."

And so they were married, in St. George's Church, in front of members of the *ton*, yes, but most importantly their families, including Georgie's mother. Georgie couldn't keep the grin from her face throughout the ceremony, nor afterward as they gathered at the Sheriden family home. Georgie had been lent a dress from Leo's sister, Sarah, who seemed most entertained by the entire affair, sitting where she was with her fiancé, a Mr. Sherwater, who Georgie had just met.

The dress hardly fit and Georgie could feel the fabric stretching around her even after Sarah's maid had used all her strength to tie her into it, but in the end, she had been declared presentable enough for the occasion.

She and Rose had taken a moment after the breakfast to stand at the side of the room — not on the outside, but, for the space of a few breaths, observers of the class they had been invited into.

"Of the four of us, would you ever have imagined that you and I would be here, married to the Belmont brothers?" Rose asked.

Georgie laughed, finally feeling unrestricted, able to show her true self, even in this home that she had been absolutely astonished by upon first arrival.

"I cannot wait to tell Alice," Georgie said, taking a sip of the champagne, wrinkling her nose at the bubbles.

"You don't think she already knows?" Rose asked with a laugh, and Georgie nodded in agreement.

"I'm actually surprised she isn't here, knocking on the door in order to determine just what is going on."

"Likely only because Benjamin didn't let her."

"Well, we will have to have a celebration of our own later on."

"Most assuredly."

Leo called Georgie to his side, surprising her by wrapping

an arm around her shoulders despite the family present in the room.

"I must apologize for surprising you with all of that. I know you think I deceived you, but I honestly never meant to. I was trying to make things right before you discovered what a bounder I was."

Georgie shook her head. "I had already learned from your father what you had done."

"My father?" He raised an eyebrow.

"She gained herself entrance to The Red Lion," Lord Sheriden said with a laugh as he joined them, and Georgie wondered at this man and the openness he displayed. He was most certainly not like any member of the nobility she had ever encountered before. "If she can do that, I suppose she can gain herself entrance to just about anywhere. Even the title of Lady Sheriden one day."

The thought took Georgie somewhat aback and for a moment she was overcome by it all — the suddenness, the change it would mean in her life. And what would happen to her job?

"I don't suppose it would be acceptable for Lady Richmond to continue working with Bow Street?" she asked with an expression somewhere between a grimace and hopefulness.

"That's something that might warrant a bit more discussion," Leo said diplomatically, and she eyed him suspiciously, but he just shook his head as though this might be a bit too much to approach his father with.

"Leo?"

They turned to find a blushing Anne standing there with her new husband. They had decided that they might as well all enjoy the breakfast that had been prepared. Lady Montrose was still beside herself, but she had been somewhat mollified when they had all been invited to the Belmont residence despite the occurrences at the church.

"Lady Anne," Leo and Georgie greeted her. "Mr. Clark."

"Congratulations," Georgie added. "I'm ever so happy for you."

"And you as well," Anne said, the picture of sincerity. "I just wanted to thank you, Leo, for everything. I never could have done this without you."

"You were admirably courageous, Lady Anne," he said, inclining his head. "I am *most* pleased this worked out for all of us."

The four of them shared a toast before Anne and Clark were on their way, and Georgie nearly jumped when Leo's breath suddenly tickled her neck.

"I think I've had enough of the same conversation over and over again," he said. "What do you say we get out of here?"

"What about my mother?"

"We can settle her in at your rooms until we find a house big enough for the three of us. You and I can share my new rooms for the time being, for there are things I must do that I wouldn't want your mother to hear."

"Leo!"

Even as he spoke the words, however, flames began to burn deep within. "Oh, very well," she said with a dramatic sigh that made him laugh as he must have realized she was not exactly averse to the idea.

"Mother?" Georgie said, approaching her, touching her arm, still shocked that she had the opportunity to do so. "Are you ready to go?"

"Yes, actually," her mother said with a slight nod. "I haven't had this much excitement in… well, in quite a few years now."

They said their farewells before Georgie changed out of

her borrowed dress, much to the Belmonts' chagrin. "But you look so beautiful," Leo's mother had attempted, before Leo had silenced her with a wave of his hand and she had nodded with a polite smile.

They had only made it down a few stairs when Drake and Marshall appeared.

"Georgie," they said after greeting Leo and Georgie's mother. "We thought you would want to know what happened to Lord Lovelace and Lord Marbury."

"Yes," she said, hurrying the rest of the way down the stairs. As eager as she was to return home with Leo, she was equally as determined to find out what had happened. Leo seemed just as interested, for he nearly beat her down the stairs in an attempt to get to the information. He looped an arm around her shoulders as though he could further protect her, although from what and who, she had no idea.

She had to admit, however, she rather liked the idea that she had someone to look out for her for a change. She had been alone for so long now, and while she had her friends and her colleagues, it wasn't quite the same as having someone who saw every aspect of her, at her most vulnerable, and loved her anyway.

"The man who actually attempted the murder — in addition to those who tried to do away with you the first time, Lord Richmond — have been taken by the magistrate and are awaiting trial. As for Lord Lovelace and Lord Marbury…"

Marshall looked a little sick as he began, "that's going to be a bit more difficult. We could not take them away from the church, of course, as it is not within our right to touch a peer. However, they will be tried before the House of Lords, for attempted murder, at the very least."

Georgie grimaced as she nodded and turned to Leo.

"What do you think will happen?"

He shook his head. "Having never sat in the House of

Lords myself, I cannot say with any certainty. From what my father says, however, I would guess that it will be pretty evenly divided. There will be those who are interested in seeing justice served, and then there will be those who won't feel that it is the place for any peer to undergo such a trial."

"Even though they tried to kill you?" Georgie asked incredulously, and Leo shrugged.

"Even though. A guilty verdict could mean execution."

"Although they will likely claim privilege."

"Most likely."

She sighed. Would this nightmare ever be over?

"Well, I suppose they will not, hopefully, try anything else in hopes of keeping their names cleared."

"That we can hope," Drake agreed.

Georgie turned to him. "Would your second, this Billings, be willing to return from the Continent?"

"If he can be found perhaps," Leo said.

"Thank you," Georgie said, looking at each of them gratefully. "For everything."

The two other detectives nodded, then looked at one another, clearly ill at ease. Georgie knew they would both have much to say in regards to her hasty wedding, although she wondered how much they would attempt with Leo's presence. She, however, was not about to let them take the coward's way out.

"Well?" she said, crossing her arms, "out with it."

Marshall pulled at his collar. "I'm not sure what you mean."

"Say what it is that you want to say."

"Ah, Georgie, we can talk later," he said, running a finger over one side of his moustache.

"I think Lady Richmond asked you a question," Leo said, and Georgie shot a look at him over her shoulder. She was only trying to have some fun with her colleagues.

"Right, Lady Richmond," Marshall said, raising a bushy red eyebrow. "It was... a pleasure working with you."

"*Was?*" Georgie repeated. "Who said I was finished?"

"Well, now that you are Lady Richmond and all..."

"I will have to speak to the magistrate, and I also have yet to discuss this with my husband," she said, looking at each of them in turn, "but I have some thoughts."

"Oh?" Drake said, his face expressionless as always, but that one syllable spoke volumes.

"Yes," she said with a curt nod. "With this case, we were discussing how valuable it would be to have someone who could move about Society. Well, like or not, I am now a part of that Society and would be an excellent informant for Bow Street."

Drake raised his brows and tilted his head.

"That's... actually not a bad idea."

"You see?" She beamed. "Now, we best be going, but we will talk to you very soon. That, I can promise you."

For she knew, as much as she loved Leo, she could never leave her work. Not completely. So it would just have to come with her.

CHAPTER 25

*L*eo was many things.

A patient man was not one of them.

He had been waiting for this woman for a long time. Longer, certainly, than she was aware of. Much longer than he had even realized himself.

All of that time that he had been attending balls, meeting young woman after young woman, none of them calling to him in a way that invited them into his heart, until he had finally considered one of them with enough affection to ask her to be his wife.

But as it turned out, they had not been meant for one another at all.

No, the woman meant for him had been a breeches-wearing detective whose laugh drew everyone near to her and caused them to join in as it was too infectious to resist.

And who was now pacing around the room, her mouth moving as she continued to review the events of the day while also recounting her thoughts on the justice system and the place of the peers within it.

"Just because a man is born a peer should not make him above the law. If he—"

"Georgie."

"—commits murder, what then? Should he be allowed to continue roaming the countryside, doing as he pleases? No, he should be—"

"Georgie."

"—tried and transported like everyone else. I'm not entirely sure how I feel about a man being put to death, although if he—"

Leo had had enough. He strode across the room, wrapped his hands around Georgie's upper arms, and kissed her, long, hard, and thoroughly. She went rigid in his arms for a moment before returning the kiss, and when he finally broke away some minutes later, he found that she was breathless and silent.

Good.

"You were trying to shut me up."

"I was."

"You don't like it when I talk?"

"Oh, Georgie," he said with a sigh, trailing a finger along the ridge of her lips. "I do like when you talk. I like it very much. Only… there are certain times when I far prefer you as a woman of action over one of talk."

She sucked her bottom lip between her teeth in a way that tugged at him somewhere else. "I see." Her eyes looked anywhere but at his — a new phenomena from Georgie.

He lifted his brow in shock. "Don't tell me you are nervous?"

"Of course not!" she scoffed, but then took a step backward.

"Georgie?"

"All right, fine!" she said, throwing her hands up in the air. "I might just be a bit nervous."

He released a low chuckle as he regarded her. There didn't seem to be much that this woman was afraid of. That she was afraid of making love to him filled him with an immense surge of power at the thought that he could be the one to help her quell her fears and find the pleasure in it all.

"Not to worry," he said huskily. "I'll make sure there is nothing to be afraid of. Now, come here."

They had returned to his rooms after they had ensured her mother was well and settled in Georgie's former home. She had many friends who had heard of her departure from Bedlam who were quite eager to see her, and while she put most of them off until the following day, one of them promised to stay with her for the night to ensure she remained well.

Georgie had been reluctant to leave her after only just seeing her again so soon, but her mother had insisted that they go and spend their first night as man and wife together.

So here they were, in Leo's rather bare apartments that his valet had, at the very least, prepared with a fire and change of bedding while Georgie was doing all she could to postpone what he had thought they both had been looking forward to for weeks.

Leo stretched his hands out toward her now, urging her closer.

She looked up at him with a hesitant smile, and he nodded encouragingly. "Do you trust me?"

"Yes, of course."

"Well, then," he said, capturing a hold of her fingers and tugging on them so she drew that much closer to him, "do you love me?"

"You know I do." The corners of her lips tugged up into a smile, just how he liked it.

"And do you desire me?"

They were but steps away from one another now, and she swallowed hard. "Yes," she said in a husky whisper.

"Then there's only one thing left to do."

He took her lips with his again, only this time, instead of just taking her breath away, he began to prepare her for what was to come without her even knowing he was doing so. He tasted, he sipped, he savored, his tongue delving, exploring, thrusting with an intensity he had never felt before, which he followed with a nibble on her lips that he extended to her earlobe before he began a sweet suckling there, causing her to gasp in shock at the sensations he knew she must be feeling.

"Oh, Leo," she said, her fingers digging into his shoulders, and he grunted his approval but was too far gone in his own desire to actually say anything practical in response.

He swept his hands up and down her back, his fingers catching on the waistcoat she had been wearing beneath her jacket. It was still feminine in nature, and the laces beneath his fingers felt as delicate as the laces of any stays. He slowly pulled them out of their buttonholes as he kissed his way from one collarbone to the next while she intertwined her fingers into his hair.

As her waistcoat slid away, he quickly dispensed of his own before catching her to him again, needing their clothes to suddenly vanish but unwilling to let her go in order to allow it to happen quickly. Instead, he had to suffer through this slow torture.

He had waited so long for her, had never thought this would ever truly come to be, and now she was here, she was his, and he knew he couldn't rush things.

"Georgie," he said as he began pulling pins from her hair, needing to see the thick tumble of curls once more, to feel them slide silkily over his fingers, "you don't know what you do to me."

"I think I have an idea," she murmured, taking his face in her palms as he began to undo the top buttons of her shirt. "I still can hardly believe that we're... we're married."

He grinned. "Believe it."

She tilted her head to the side, and he wondered where her smile had gone.

"You do know that it's never going to be easy between us? I know in the vows I had to promise to be obedient, but..."

She winced and he chuckled.

"I love you because of the woman you are, Georgie, and no other reason. If I wanted an obedient wife, I could have found any number of them littering the *ton*. But that's not what I wanted. I wanted you. Now, if nothing else, would you agree to that?"

She looked up to the ceiling as though she was considering it.

"I suppose I can."

She couldn't help herself then — she laughed, long and loud, and he joined in. He used to think he had known it all, and it was only upon his rescue that he realized how wrong he had been.

But there was one thing that he did know for certain — he could spend his entire life trying, but he would never get enough of Georgie.

Her buttons undone, she drew her shirt over her head, and he followed suit before picking her up and tossing her on the bed, climbing on himself and capturing her between his arms. He bent his head to kiss her again, before he could no longer resist becoming reacquainted with her breasts, which were crying out for his attention.

While she was not as voluptuous as some women he had known before, he couldn't overcome his admiration for the sculpted strength of her body, and those round, pert breasts that fit perfectly in his hands were all that he could ever ask for.

"You're beautiful," he said before bending and worshipping her with his mouth as she groaned and arched up against him.

"More," she panted, and who was Leo to deny her?

He unfastened the breeches she wore before shucking his trousers, and upon the shock of the contact of their skin on one another, he nearly froze at the exquisite pleasure.

She was his — now and for the rest of their lives. As much as he knew he had all the time in the world, his body was telling him otherwise.

He ran his hands down from her breasts, across her taut abdomen, his thumbs on the middle of her stomach as his hands splayed wide across her hips. He bent his head, his lips running down the groove in the middle of her stomach, his tongue dipping into her belly button, causing her to giggle, a sound he hadn't heard from her before. He chuckled softly before he continued his descent, until his lips found her and she sucked in a breath, her back arching up off the bed as she threw her head back.

Leo reached a finger within her, then another, finding her ready for him, and he leaned up, looking her intently in the eyes as he placed a kiss on her forehead.

"You're amazing."

"You might be if you ever begin," she said wryly and he laughed — until she reached down and took him in her hand, and then he was no longer laughing.

"Don't, Georgie."

"Why not?" she asked, moving her hand up and down slowly, sending him spiralling out from the slow torture. "Don't tell me that you aren't enjoying this?"

"Oh, I'm enjoying it all right," he replied, his words coming out in a hiss. "I'm enjoying it all too much."

Finally he couldn't take it anymore, and he pulled her hand away as gently as he could before lowering himself down to her entrance. He positioned himself just outside as he leaned down and kissed her while moving his thumb over her nub of nerves.

She hissed in pain when he first thrust into her, and he stopped once he was inside, sweat beading on his brow as he allowed her to become used to him.

She dug her fingers into his hips and he heaved a sigh of relief before he started moving, slowly at first, looking deep into Georgie's eyes as he joined with her — his wife. The woman he would spend the rest of his life with.

Georgie being Georgie, she matched him in rhythm, not letting him take charge, and what she lacked in experience she made up for in enthusiasm.

He stroked her in time with his thrusts until suddenly she tightened around him, at first squeezing her eyes shut but then opening them to stare into his just as he reached his climax and spilled his seed into her, his breath ragged when he finally collapsed beside her.

She threw an arm over her forehead as she looked over at him, and he couldn't help a smug grin.

"Aren't you glad we left the wedding breakfast?"

She punched him in the arm, and he laughed, knowing that he would always find love, laughter, and humor with Georgie — well worth the fact that he would likely also be forever worrying about her safety.

"I love you," he said, resting his forehead against hers.

"And I love you."

EPILOGUE

"Come in, come in," Georgie opened the door as wide as her smile as she welcomed her guests. Perry and Rose had arrived first, and up the walk she could see Madeline and Drake alighting from the carriage along with Alice and Benjamin.

How strange, that for so long she had considered these women so far above her in station and now she was welcoming them to her home as the wife of a viscount.

"Thank you for having us," Alice said once they entered and had passed the butler — Georgie could hardly believe she had a butler — their cloaks.

"Of course," Georgie said with a warm smile. "It's the first time I've ever really had a home that has a dining room table big enough to fit guests around."

She was wearing a dress tonight for the occasion — a reality that she had become much more used to since marrying Leo. Not that he didn't enjoy when she wore her breeches, but she had been invited to more polite events in the last month than she had in her entire life. Most they turned down, but they did have an obligation to represent the family now and again.

Georgie would spend most of the evenings standing at the side of the room, surveying the guests, as she was still learning how to dance — a feat she had thought she would never accomplish but it seemed her athletic abilities were helpful in more ways than fighting off unwanted attackers. She would partake in the odd waltz, if her partner was capable enough to lead her through the steps.

"Your home is lovely," Madeline said as she walked around the front parlor. Georgie nodded graciously.

"My mother has been helpful in decorating and preparing it to be fit for company," she said.

"You must be so pleased to have her home," Rose said with a soft smile. It was the final night that Rose and Perry would be in London before they returned to Lyme Regis — the place where they had found one another... and happiness.

"I most certainly am," Georgie said with a grin as ladies and gentlemen alike all moved into the drawing room.

"Georgie," Drake appeared at her elbow. "Do you have a moment?"

"I do," she said with a nod, stepping to the side, unsure of whether or not she should be worried — with Drake, one never entirely knew as his expression was always so vague. "Is everything all right?"

"It is," he said with a nod. "But the magistrate has need of your help," he said in a low voice.

"Oh, do tell," she said enthusiastically, pleased to hear it. She had approached the Bow Street magistrate with her suggestion that while she might have more difficulty continuing with them in her current capacity, perhaps she could be of help in a different way, now that she would have more access to higher Society.

"There is a thief that has been targeting homes of the nobility — sneaking into bedrooms during parties and balls and making off with jewellery and other items of particular value."

"Really?" she said, her eyes widening. "Why have I not heard anything of this?"

"People are trying to keep it quiet," he said, "not wanting to be embarrassed that one of their own guests could possibly have anything to do with it, or that there was such a breach of security in their own homes."

"What would you like me to do?"

"Next time you're at a party, keep an eye out. See if anyone is habitually going off alone, if anyone leaves early. Be observant."

"That, I can do," she promised.

"But Georgie, whatever you do, do not go after anyone alone, understand?"

"Of course," she said, feeling a presence behind her, knowing without looking that Leo was there. She swallowed hard, wondering what he would think of such a plan.

She glanced backward and noted that his sea-green eyes had darkened slightly.

"Listen to Drake, Georgie," he said. "Don't put yourself in danger."

She was about to argue, to tell him that she could look after herself, but then she saw that flash in his eyes, telling her that he was not trying to order her about, but was simply worried about her, and her heart melted a bit.

"Very well," she promised. "I will be careful. But I *will* find the information you need."

"Of course you will," Drake said. "Now, my wife is giving me that look that tells me I am to leave work alone for the evening. Shall we rejoin everyone?"

"Absolutely. Actually," she and Leo exchanged a glance,

"what do you say we all have a game of billiards? Leo and Perry were not present last time and have been itching for the chance to try themselves."

Everyone in agreement, they followed them down the hallway of the townhouse they had moved into just a few weeks before. There were still rooms that required furnishings and décor, but it was theirs and they had found all the happiness they could ever ask for within its four walls.

"Shall our winners from last time go first?" Alice asked, waving her hand toward Madeline and Drake, even as Madeline laughed in protest.

"That was just beginner's luck."

"There is only one way to determine that," Alice said, challenge in her voice, and Madeline rolled her eyes and sighed at her old friend as she insisted that Drake break the table.

They faced off first against Alice and Benjamin, but this time Alice was not to be bested, and they won handily. Madeline didn't seem to mind, nor did she protest when her husband tried to help her once more.

"Who is next? Rose and Perry?"

Rose and Perry agreed, although neither looked particularly thrilled about a game of billiards. "Perry's never really been one for games," Leo said in his deep voice right beside Georgie's ear, which never failed to cause shivers all the way down her spine.

"No?"

"He doesn't have the competitive spirit."

Georgie's lips curled up. "Hmm, I wonder who received all of that in the family."

Leo laughed, causing the attention of the rest of the room to turn toward them. They had played their own fair share of games, and it was hard to say just who came out the victor the majority of the time.

Alice and Benjamin quickly beat Rose and Perry, whose hearts just weren't in the game but seemed to be more wrapped up in one another.

Leo and Georgie shared a grin as they stepped up to the table.

"Let me guess," Alice said, raising an eyebrow. "You've been practicing?"

"Something like that," Georgie said nonchalantly, as they heard Perry snort from behind them.

"I'm not sure I like the sounds of that," Benjamin said from across the table.

"We had a billiards room in our house growing up," Perry said nonchalantly, not caring about the glare Leo sent his way. "It was Leo's favorite room."

"Didn't you say there was an old table at the orphanage where you lived?" Rose asked with a smile of her own as Georgie prepared her cue.

Alice and Benjamin looked on in horror as Georgie began the game, clearing half the balls off the table.

"You're up," she said when it was Alice's turn, and Alice took on a determined expression as she stepped to the table and did her very best to run it.

But she couldn't quite make it, and then Leo finished off the game before Benjamin even got a turn.

"That was not fair," Alice said, facing Georgie with hands on her hips, and Georgie laughed. "Probably not," she agreed. "What do you say we have dinner and then we can return and play again?"

Alice considered the proposition for a moment before she agreed.

"Very well. But now that we are prepared, do not consider yourself so fortunate."

Georgie agreed, but once Alice had left she looked at Leo

and began to laugh. They lingered for a moment before following their guests.

"We are lucky, aren't we?" Georgie mused.

"To have such friends?"

"Yes," she said with a nod. "Around whom I can be myself, and I don't have to worry about fitting in."

"Do you worry about that?" he asked her, concern in her eyes.

"I do sometimes," she said, "Although part of me feels that perhaps more people are on our side than we realized, especially after the House of Lords convicted Lord Marbury and Lord Lovelace."

"That was astonishing," he said, taking her hands in his, and looking down at her. "But you have a way of bringing people in close to you, a way that I have not seen in anyone else. It is why you have always been so good at what you do, why you are the most incredible woman."

"Oh, stop," Georgie said, reaching in and pulling him close, "before you talk me into leaving our guests and taking you upstairs."

He raised an eyebrow. "You should never have said that."

When he leaned down to pretend to hoist her up over his shoulder, she swatted at him, and they laughed until he nuzzled her neck and whispered, "later," before they did continue on and join their guests for dinner.

As she sat back and stared at the dinner table before her, Georgie knew that while she still didn't quite remember the order of the courses nor which cutlery accompanied which course, what she did know was that, even in this world where there should be such a divide between where she came from and where she had ended up, here, in this circle of people who had become so close to her, she had found a place of love and acceptance.

And with Leo, who was even now taking her fingers under the table, choosing to sit next to her rather than across from her, she had found love in the most unlikeliest of places.

She met his blue-green eyes now, the eyes where she had always found such a sense of peace, and when he grinned at her, she returned it right back to him.

One thing was certain — their adventure was only just beginning.

THE END

THE ART OF STEALING A DUKE'S HEART

Preview the first book of the exciting new series

A SNEAK PEEK...

"*Y*ou can try as hard as you like, but you will never blend in."

Calliope fixed an annoyed gaze on her sister, who so easily slipped into the shadows unnoticed that Calli hadn't even seen her approach.

"We are supposed to be avoiding one another."

"That's what Arie said, yes, but then Arie isn't here, now is he?"

One corner of Calli's lips tugged up into a smile. Diana was right, but while she had always been the forgotten one, she was also, in her own way, the most rebellious.

While Calli would far prefer to be recognized for standing out rather than slapping back.

"You're supposed to be searching the house by now," Diana said from the corner of her mouth. "Why are you still here in the ballroom?"

Calli sighed as she turned from her sister, staring back out across the dance floor in front of them, at the swirls of colorful gowns draping the women's bodies, and the dashing gentlemen who held them in close embraces.

"I just… wanted to watch the dancing. I've never seen a waltz like this before."

"We learned it, though."

It was true. They had been part of all of their lessons. Lessons on how to be one of these people, how to fit in and make everyone believe their lies.

"But to dance it, here, in such a room, with the angels watching from paintings above, surrounded by pillars, my feet on marble, it would be like I was dancing among the gods and goddesses themselves."

Diana choked out a bark of laughter at Calli's fanciful words, and Calli found her face growing hot at the fact that she had actually said them aloud.

"This is not your world, Calli. It never will be. We are here for one purpose, and one purpose only. Do you understand?"

Calli gave a quick nod before turning from the scene in front of her. Diana was right. She had a job to do. One she could hardly believe that Arie had actually trusted her with. Calli smoothed her hand down the grey muslin of her skirts, created for this very function. She was to fit in, to make all believe she was a companion, not a debutante who would be expected to be making her acquaintance with young gentlemen or stepping onto the floor in a waltz.

"Besides," Diana said, her voice softening as she stared at the woman who was her sister in nearly every sense of the word, "if you were to step out onto that dance floor, every person – man or woman – would not be able to help but notice you. You would be the talk of Society."

"I would not," Calli said with a roll of her eyes, looking down at her inconspicuous garment. They had swept back all of her riotous black curls, doing their utmost to tame them into a harsh knot at the back of her head, while her face was devoid of anything that might highlight her prominent features.

"You told Arie you could do this," Diana continued. "So are you going to follow through, or not?"

"Of course I am," Calli said, straightening her spine. She was determined to show her brother that she was as capable as any of them at accomplishing success in the family business. "I will back."

Diana nodded in approval. "I'll keep watch."

Calli slipped through the crowds, closing her eyes for a moment as she reviewed the map of the grand London townhouse in her mind. She would start in the drawing rooms, then move back through the house. She was sure to eventually find her quarry. She just had to make sure she did so unnoticed.

The key to accessing entry, she reminded herself, hearing Arie's words in her head, *is to convince everyone around you that you belong.*

She nodded with a small smile to the maid she passed as she walked through the foyer, and the girl nearly ran away. Calli wondered if she was supposed to remain hidden from the guests.

While each of her siblings possessed their own extraordinary skill, they had all learned the ways of the nobility so that they would fit into their surroundings when the occasion called for it. Calli had never quite grasped the way the upper crust treated those who they considered below them – especially the people who worked for them.

But no matter. That was why she should feel no guilt over what she was about to do.

Besides, if she did her job correctly, no one would ever be the wiser, and the Duke could continue to enjoy his fine artwork.

She cracked open the first door, finding the drawing

room ready for visitors, but currently unoccupied. She slipped in, rounding the room and finding plenty of paintings that would fetch a good price, but none that she was looking for.

A parlor and dining room later, she was still without success.

Trying to not panic, reminding herself that she was trained for this and would be just fine, she pushed open the last door before the end of the small corridor.

And found herself swallowed by the darkness of a decidedly masculine room.

While embers still burned in the grate, this room was not ready for visitors, and Calli received the impression more than ever that she was trespassing. She crossed to the desk, where a candle awaited in a surprisingly plain small candle holder. She lit the wick before holding it high as she crossed the room, beginning at the door as she made a slow circle, casting the flickering light upon the walls.

This was never going to work, she thought, shaking her head. Even if she found the painting, she would never be able to study it. Not in this light. Most certainly not with enough detail to ever do it justice.

She sighed. She would have to return and tell Arie she had failed. She could already see the disappointment on his face as he sighed and told her that he never should have trusted her. If only there was another way.

Just as Calli was about to turn to the door, color glimmered from across the room, where her light had reflected off a painting on the far wall. Her heart began to drum excitedly in her chest. There it was.

She began to step closer to the painting, when the door swung open, freezing her footsteps. She closed her eyes, wishing that by doing so she could hide completely, but she was far too old to believe such a thing.

She turned, ever so slowly, waiting to see who had caught her in their trap.

Only to find two blond-haired, blue-eyed children, their cherubic chubby faces seemingly having come to life from the murals in the ballroom, staring at her with grins on their faces.

~~~~~

THIS HAD BEEN A MISTAKE.

Although, so were most of the decisions Jonathan had made in his three decades so far on earth.

None, perhaps, had such serious repercussions as the throwaway promise he had made to his sister.

"Of course, I'll look after them," he had said when she had asked if he would take care of her twin children if anything were to ever happen to her. "I wouldn't expect you to trust any other more than your brother."

At the time, he had never expected that his exuberant, carefree sister was actually planning her own departure, that she was leaving her children, already devoid of a father who had died too young, for a life of adventure. It still caused rage to rise within him every time he remembered reading the note. The note that explained she was running away to America, but that it was too much to take her children. That she was never meant to be a mother, and would Jonathan please look after them?

Jonathan's own mother had been so beside herself that Jonathan could do nothing but agree. He had hired the best of governesses, determined to provide them a home and a proper education, but knew nothing more of what he was to do.

But now, his mother was insisting that the children required a mother figure. This ball was supposed to help him find one. Of course, her mother herself, who far preferred Bath, had not even bothered to attend, but it was much for the better.

For the thought of tying himself to one of these women for the rest of his life made him ill. None of them seemed capable of becoming a mother, most of the young ladies vying for his attention little more than children themselves. And the twins were not exactly the most... docile of creatures.

Speaking of the little hellions...

He caught a glimpse of a blond head from across the ball-room, and it was not the elaborately coiffed hair of one of the young ladies. No, this was wild, bouncing blond hair that was running away after being caught somewhere it didn't belong.

"Damn it," he said, his grip on his glass so strong he nearly crushed it.

"Everything all right, Hargreave?"

Belatedly, Jonathan remembered his friend, Marcus Davenport, who was standing beside him, surveying the room in front of him with a smirk on his face. He had always been the carefree sort, a trait that Jonathan envied. For Jonathan cared all too much.

"Fine," he said tersely, knocking back his drink before setting in on the empty tray of a passing servant. "I must go attend to something."

"Would that 'something' be a precocious six-year-old?"

Jonathan eyed him sharply. If Davenport had seen either of the children, then he couldn't be sure who else had witnessed their presence.

"They must have outwitted Mrs. Blonsky again," he said

with a sigh. "She told me she couldn't keep up. I should have listened to her."

"Why do you have your housekeeper watching them?" Davenport asked, one of his black eyebrows lifted.

"The new governess failed to arrive this morning."

"How many is that now?"

Jonathan eyed him sharply, sensing the amusement in his friend's voice. But this was no laughing matter. He had spent far too many hours hiring governesses, and then listening to their complaints as they quit. He was through with it. At least a wife wouldn't be able to leave the situation.

Davenport was still waiting for an answer.

"Six." Jonathan sighed.

"Six! One a month, then."

"So it is. I'll be back."

He set out of the ballroom, hoping that the little monkeys hadn't invaded the ballroom itself, but were somewhere on the periphery. Not sensing them or any commotion made by them in the big room, he continued through the ground floor of the house, observing each room as he went, interrupting one scandalous affair that he basically ignored before moving on.

Perhaps the children had actually returned to the nursery, or Mrs. Blonsky had found them, he considered hopefully, already knowing that the idea was too good to be true.

A peal of laughter confirmed that.

He hurried down the corridor to the study, his mind already running over all the kinds of trouble they could find themselves in down there. He tried to remember if he had locked his desk drawers. He was sure he had, and even if they did manage to break into his ledgers and destroy them, his man-of-business had another set, but still… there was only one man Jonathan *completely* trusted.

Himself.

Annoyed at the entire event, the disappearing governess, the fact that his niece and nephew couldn't even give him one night in which they would stay out of trouble, he was not entirely subtle when he pushed open the door, stepping through the opening with determination to end this madness and demonstrate to his niece and nephew exactly what happened when they disobeyed.

Only to find himself momentarily speechless.

For there, sitting demurely in front of the two chairs before his desk, were two little angels, gazing raptly, silently – for once – at the woman before them.

She spoke with exuberance, her hands flying in front of her, her face full of expressions as she spoke of animals and goddesses and nonsense tales.

The children seemed to be enjoying every minute of it.

So much so, that they hadn't even noticed him. Not yet.

Until suddenly, the woman stopped mid-sentence, turning toward him with her hands still lifted, her mouth rounded in an O.

After the moment in which she was seemingly suspended in time, she threw back the chair so quickly she nearly knocked it over before running a few steps backward.

"My lord, I'm so very sorry, I—"

"Your Grace."

"Pardon me?" Her cheeks flushed a most becoming shade of red.

"The correct address for a duke is 'Your Grace.'"

"Yes, Your Grace, of course. My apologies. I did not mean to sit in your chair, it was just that the children told me they were not tired, and I thought perhaps I would tell them a bedtime story. It always used to help me, although ideally they would actually be in their beds and—"

Jonathan took a breath, closing his eyes for a moment as he held up a hand to quell her flow of words.

"You are late, Miss Donahue."

"Pardon me?" she said again, her eyes wide to reveal the most stunning shade of violet-blue he had ever seen.

"I said that you are late. You are Miss Donahue, are you not?"

"I... Y-yes."

"Very well. Welcome. Not only are you late, but you have arrived in the middle of a house party, and you are entertaining the children from my chair in my study. But, if you happen to suit with the children, all of that will be overlooked."

"I—what?" She looked at him in surprise, and he wondered if most employers were stricter. Perhaps he would have to rectify that issue.

"Children," he said to the twins, "meet your new governess."

* * *

THE ART of Stealing a Duke's Heart is now available for pre-order on Amazon.

ALSO BY ELLIE ST. CLAIR

The Bluestocking Scandals

Designs on a Duke

Inventing the Viscount

Discovering the Baron

The Valet Experiment

Writing the Rake

Risking the Detective

A Noble Excavation

A Gentleman of Mystery

For a full list of all of Ellie's books, please see

www.elliestclair.com/books.

ABOUT THE AUTHOR

Ellie has always loved reading, writing, and history. For many years she has written short stories, non-fiction, and has worked on her true love and passion -- romance novels.

In every era there is the chance for romance, and Ellie enjoys exploring many different time periods, cultures, and geographic locations. No matter when or where, love can always prevail. She has a particular soft spot for the bad boys of history, and loves a strong heroine in her stories.

Ellie and her husband love nothing more than spending time at home with their two sons and Husky cross. Ellie can typically be found at the lake in the summer, pushing the stroller all year round, and, of course, with her computer in her lap or a book in hand.

She also loves corresponding with readers, so be sure to contact her!

www.elliestclair.com
ellie@elliestclair.com

Ellie St. Clair's Ever Afters Facebook Group